Humleby Farm 2

Will Sofie Have To Choose?

Malin Stehn

Will Sofie Have
To Choose?

ISBN: 978-1-934983-14-0

Stabenfeldt, Inc.
225 Park Avenue South
New York, NY 10003
www.pony4kids.com

Available exclusively through PONY.

For Tisbe, an angel in cat heaven.

One head, four legs

It was an almost impossibly beautiful evening. The setting sun made the sky glow in pink and orange. The wispy, bluish-purple clouds looked like they'd been painted on with a large brush. The air was completely still and the swallows were flying so high that they looked more like insects than birds.

Sofie was sitting in the grass next to Speedy's paddock, watching her favorite horse. The gelding was standing by the fence, grazing contentedly. The last rays of sunshine barely reached the paddock, and the chestnut trotting horse's shadow was melting into the shadow of the lean-to nearby. Sofie thought to herself that there probably wasn't a more beautiful place on Earth than Humleby. And there probably wasn't a horse more beautiful than Speedy.

"This place is completely dead! I don't know how you can stand it."

Next to Sofie, her older sister Emma had just broken the comfortable silence.

"I think it's alright," Sofie answered. She didn't want her big sister to think she was too enthusiastic. Just a month ago Sofie had hated Humleby, horses and her whole existence. That's why she still wasn't completely used to saying that she actually liked the country life.

"We have to get to town tomorrow!" Emma sounded desperate. "We can't just hang around here all day. I'll ask Dad if we can borrow the car, and then you can show me the best stores." She looked happy at the thought.

Sofie realized that she'd barely gone into town since her family had come to Sweden about four weeks ago. Right after the move she had, against her will, started a summer job at Humleby Farm.

But gradually things had changed. Tina, one of the grooms, had made Sofie curious about the big animals, and one day, when the former Swedish Trotting Derby winner, Speedy Legend, came to the stable, Sofie's attitude toward horses changed completely.

Speedy wasn't just an unusually beautiful horse. He was also new at Humleby Farm – just as she was. Sofie had felt a bond with the chestnut trotter right away, and with that also a feeling of responsibility to make sure that he liked his new home.

At first Sofie's cousin Isabelle had been really mean to her, but now Isabelle and Sofie were friends and Sofie liked her job just fine. She was even getting used to the fact that she thought about horses even when she wasn't working. It still was a weird feeling, but she'd accepted that she, for some strange reason, actually *liked* the big animals.

Humleby Farm, one of the country's biggest trotting stables, was owned by Sofie's mother's brother, Uncle Tommy and his wife Aunt Maggie. Tommy Sandberg was a well-known name in the trotting business, and he was considered to be one of the best trotting trainers in all of Sweden.

Sofie's hatred of her new job from the start was partly due to the fact that 15-year-old Isabelle had done everything to make her life as horrible as possible. And also partly due to the fact that she'd been afraid of horses all her life. The only reason Sofie had gone to the stable at all during those first weeks was to make money; money that she was going to use to pay for a trip back to her old home, London, to see her best friend Jojo.

Early mornings and long days at the stable meant that she hadn't had that much time to go into town, and the strange thing was that she didn't miss her city life all that much. She did, however, miss Jojo, but that was a different matter altogether...

"Right?" Emma persisted. "Wouldn't it be fun if we could go into town and do some shopping tomorrow?"

Sofie was jolted from her thoughts.

"You only just got here today," she pointed out. "Don't you want to see the rest of the village first?"

Emma had stayed in London when the rest of the Lindquist family moved back to Sweden. She was a college student, and she was visiting Humleby for a few weeks during her summer break.

"The rest of the village?" Emma snorted. "I've been here before, so I know what little there is to see. And I really want to go shopping!"

Sofie wondered how someone coming right from London could want to go shopping in tiny Malmö.

"Well, we'll see what dad says about the car. It's been a while since you drove, right?"

"I drove a car last week," Emma informed her little sister.

"On the 'wrong' side of the road, yes."

"*That* doesn't matter. I've driven a car in right-hand traffic before."

Instead of reminding Emma that she, during the family's last visit to Sweden, had gone against the traffic in a rotary and almost given their father a heart attack, she said, "Isn't he nice?" She was looking at Speedy, who lifted his head, studying the sisters with his dark, wise eyes.

"Who?" Emma looked at the gravel road between the paddocks. "We're the only ones here!"

Sofie sighed.

"Speedy, of course!" She pointed to the chestnut in front of them.

"Oh." Emma considered Speedy for a while. "Well, he looks like a horse," she said. "One head, four legs."

Sofie pulled up a fistful of grass and threw it at her sister. "Take this for four legs!"

"Aaah! What are you doing?" Emma shook her head to get rid of the grass that had stuck in her dark hair. Then she quickly pulled up a handful of the tall grass and counterattacked.

Soon, the war was underway. The grass tufts flew accompanied by violent giggling. At last, Emma was straddling Sofie's stomach, with one hand around her little sister's wrist and an earthy handful of grass in the other.

"Surrender!" she screamed, lowering the tuft threateningly toward Sofie's face.

Sofie laughed until she cried, and gasped for breath under her sister's weight. She shook her head.

"Surrender! Or you'll have to eat this!" Emma growled, eyes sparkling with laughter.

By now, the grass was less than an inch away from

8

Sofie's mouth. She turned her head to the left so that she wouldn't get dirt in her nostrils.

"Eat it!" Emma continued, but gave up when Sofie managed to worm out of her grip and throw herself to the side.

They got up and started brushing dirt from their clothes.

"I'm glad that you're here," Sofie said as she put on her sandals. "I've missed having someone to fight with," she smiled.

"Likewise," her big sister replied, smoothing down her sleeveless top. "But I still don't understand how you can stand it here. It's so quiet! Listen!"

They stood in silence for a while, listening to the country sounds. The only thing that could be heard was the sound of hooves as Speedy rushed across the paddock and then a neigh from his friend Sky. Far off in the distance, you could make out a dull roar from the expressway, and in the moss behind them hundreds of frogs held a late-evening concert.

"I like it," Sofie answered. "But I thought it was creepy at first."

The sisters started walking toward the gravel road and Sofie turned around.

"Bye, Speedy, I'll see you tomorrow!" she called.

Speedy's ears revealed that he'd registered her goodbye, but he didn't lift his head. He kept munching the fresh grass instead. Dusk had fallen and the only things that could be seen were the silhouettes of the two horses at the far end of the paddock.

"So, you're into horses now? Really?" Emma sounded skeptical. "Mom said something about that on the phone," she continued, "but I didn't take her seriously. I thought she was pulling my leg. Wow, Sofie! It's been four weeks since you left London and you were *afraid* of horses then!"

"I know..." Sofie shrugged. "Maybe 'into horses' is a bit of an exaggeration, but... I like them, somehow. The horses, that is."

"You must be incredibly easy to influence!" Despite the darkness, Sofie could see her sister shaking her head indignantly. "Maybe it's an age thing?" Emma continued, suddenly sounding as if she were forty instead of twenty.

"Do you have anything against me liking horses?" Sofie was getting annoyed. Why should she have to defend herself?

Emma didn't answer right away. After a while, she said, "No, not really. I guess I'm just not used to it. It doesn't really feel like you're you, if you catch my drift..."

And who am I? Sofie thought to herself. *Was I someone else when I lived in London?*

It was difficult to get the concepts straight. Deep down she still felt just like the old Sofie, the Sofie who lived in London and liked nice clothes, dancing, drawing and listening to music. And she still thought all those things were great, really. It was just that she'd found yet another interest: horses. Maybe she really was easily influenced. Sofie decided she'd rather think of herself as adaptable.

Someone who lived in Humleby and hated horses would probably find life rather hard because there were more horses than humans in the little village. And that's why it was easier to get used to the four-legged animals than keep on not liking them.

To be completely honest with herself, Sofie was still a little afraid of horses. Thirteen years of fear didn't just disappear in four weeks. But the fear she felt now was a different kind than the one she'd felt before.

10

The old fear had been completely unfounded and terrible. She'd felt as if every horse in the whole world was out to get her, and she'd refused to go near them. The new fear was more about the animals' size and intelligence. She realized the horses didn't mean her any harm. Generally a horse behaved badly only when it was scared or in pain. For example, Speedy had been very troublesome when he arrived at Humleby Farm less than a month ago. He'd kicked and bitten and been restless. Rumor was that the gelding had been badly treated by his previous owner, and once he arrived at Humleby Farm, they had discovered that he was suffering from a boil on his hoof. As soon as the boil ruptured and Speedy had gotten used to his new environment, he'd turned into a completely different horse. Now he was almost as calm as the stable's oldest, calmest horse, the good-natured Sky.

"I'm me," answered Sofie. And went on. "If you catch my drift," she imitated her sister, shoving her lightly in the side.

"I think I do." Emma countered with a hard push that sent Sofie stumbling onto the uneven gravel road.

"And you're definitely still you." Sofie knew that her sister had a satisfied grin on her face; she could just make out a faint row of teeth in the darkness.

Former best friend?

"Fine, fine!" Stefan Lindquist held the car keys, dangling from a key ring, in front of his older daughter's face. "But I want both the car and my children to come home unharmed."

Emma snatched the keys from his hand.

"Of course!" she chirped and kissed her father on the cheek. "Piece of cake."

"Help me, Elizabeth!" Stefan threw his arms out and looked pleadingly at the girls' mother. "What is it about Emma that makes me give in every time?"

"Female guile and good persuasion skills," laughed Elizabeth, who was wiping the crumbs from breakfast off the kitchen table. "She got it from me," she added, winking at Emma.

Female guile and good nagging skills, Sofie thought unkindly. She decided to try to get along with Emma now that they were going to town together.

Sofie thought it would be really fun to go shopping with her sister. She needed a new pair of jeans, and trying on new clothes was always better when you had an advisor.

Also, Emma was the most up-to-date member of her family when it came to fashion and trends.

Elizabeth wrung the water from a rag and then wiped her hands on a towel.

"Shouldn't you ask Isabelle if she wants to go with you?" she asked, looking at her daughters. Sofie stiffened. One of the reasons Isabelle had been so mean toward Sofie in her first weeks at the stable had to do with Emma. According to Isabelle, Emma had always ignored her during family reunions. And Isabelle, who had always admired her older, more urbane cousin, had felt pushed aside and neglected. She had taken those feelings out on Sofie when her cousin started her new job.

Now, however, everything was calm on that front. Isabelle had apologized and Sofie had forgiven her, but making Emma and Isabelle hang out wasn't especially tempting. She wouldn't mind waiting.

"Isabelle's working today," Sofie hurried to say. Which was, incidentally, true.

"She works Saturdays?" Emma looked surprised.

Sofie sighed. Sometimes Emma was really dense.

"Horses are hungry on Saturdays, and Sundays too."

"Well, obviously. I *get* that," Emma replied, slightly annoyed. "But I thought Emma – the owner's daughter – could maybe get weekends off. Don't they have employees?"

"Several," Sofie confirmed. "But Tommy, Aunt Maggie, Isabelle and Daniel do most of the work."

Daniel was Isabelle's big brother.

"And it's a family business," Stefan interjected. "They try to do as much as possible themselves, because employees cost so much."

13

"Thanks for the information, but I don't want an economics lesson." Emma rattled the car keys. "I want to go to town!"

"Promise me you'll drive carefully." Stefan had worry lines across his forehead.

"I've already said I will!" Emma smiled. "Isabelle can come another time," she said to her mother. "Let's go."

"Sure," Sofie answered lightly, but inwardly, she prayed the trip wouldn't end in chaos.

"Oops!" Emma exclaimed when their dad's silver gray Audi sputtered and stopped for the second time in a minute. "This car is hopeless! There's got to be something wrong with the clutch!" She rushed the engine, and the car jumped a few feet before settling into a normal speed again.

They had just passed Speedy's paddock, but Sofie didn't dare take her eyes off the road even for a second. She had forgotten just how terrifying it was being in a car with her big sister behind the wheel.

"That's probably mostly because of the driver," she couldn't help saying.

"Quiet!" Emma snapped. She was obviously stressed. "I drive really well if it's a normal car." She punched the black plastic above the dashboard, as if that would somehow make the Audi obey her better.

Sofie was about to say that there had been nothing wrong with the car when she and her mom had gone to the airport the day before, but she kept her mouth shut. She didn't want to make her sister even more agitated. Instead she stared at the road in front of them, fearing what would happen when they got closer to the center of town and roads with more traffic. So far, they were only on the outskirts of town.

On her right was Humleby church, looking down at them from its hill. Beyond the trees on their left-hand side was a practice trotting course, where the trotters in their area could polish their form before races.

Sofie knew that Speedy would soon have to show what he could do. So far, her uncle had just worked with Speedy to make sure he was ready to race. The gelding had been in a very bad state when he got to Humleby Farm, but just in the last week he had shown that he was just about ready for a test race.

Tina had tried explaining the rules of trotting to Sofie. She had also told her about all the different demands that had to be met before a horse could participate in a bigger race. After the lecture, Sofie had felt confused. The only thing she'd really understood was that Speedy had to participate in a qualifying race before he could compete for the big prizes again.

And it was the big prizes that Tommy and Speedy's owner, Axel, were hoping for.

"Darn it!"

The car had stalled again. The girls were at an intersection with traffic lights, and the drivers behind them were honking angrily.

"Take it easy!" Emma growled, turned the key, and floored it. The Audi shot through the intersection like an arrow. "This car is driving me crazy," she hissed as they neared the center of town, going much too fast.

The only thing missing now to make this day a perfect mess is us for us to get a speeding ticket, Sofie thought, desperately holding on to her seat.

"I have to drive this fast," Emma said, as if she'd heard Sofie's thoughts. "If I don't, the car's going to stall again."

Sofie was relieved when they parked in one of the town's biggest parking garages and stepped out onto the sidewalk. Emma had, against all odds, managed to get the Audi into the building and park without scratching it or crashing into any of the concrete pillars.

"Here we are!" she exclaimed, satisfied, dropping the car keys into her purse. "That's step one. Now for step two. Toward the shops!"

Sofie couldn't help smiling. Her sister had a temper – but at least her fits of rage passed quickly. Hurrying, they headed toward the nearest mall.

"Aaah!" Emma sank down onto a sparsely designed café chair and stretched her legs. "I'm beat!"

Sofie swallowed a mouthful of her orange juice, agreeing.

"We've been standing and walking for almost three hours," she stated with a quick look at the clock hanging above the café counter.

The girls had decided to take a break from shopping and were now sitting at a café, stylishly furnished, in the center of town. The chairs were hard, with low backrests, but it was still nice to sit down for a while.

"I'm so happy with our loot!" Emma gestured toward all the bags that were placed in a large pile on the floor. Then she leaned forward, stirring her smoothie.

Sofie was happy with her purchases too. She'd found two new pairs of jeans that felt a little more fun than the old worn ones hanging in her closet back home. She'd also had enough money for a short-sleeved top, a magazine and some candy. She looked forward to throwing herself on the couch with the candy and the magazine when they got home.

"So what do you think of the town?" she asked her sister. "Did it look like this when you were younger?"

"Not at all!" Emma swept her arm toward the sidewalk outside the big window. "It was much more boring ten years ago. There were no outdoor cafés at all, and not as many shops."

"But it doesn't compare to London, right?"

"No... but I think it's okay," Emma replied, taking a bite of her grilled sandwich. "I mean, you can find everything here, and everything's close, not like London. Besides..." She chewed a piece of mozzarella. "... I've been studying like crazy the past few weeks. I've almost forgotten what my favorite stores in London look like."

"You poor thing," Sofie answered, with just a little sarcasm in her voice.

Emma let her sister's comment go without a comeback.

"Have you heard from Jojo?" she asked instead.

Sofie had been waiting for Emma to start asking questions about Jojo. And it pained her that she couldn't reply, *Sure! We e-mail each other every day and we've planned everything we're going to do when I visit in August.*

"Yeah..." Sofie drew her answer out. "A while ago."

Emma looked up from her sandwich, and looked carefully at her little sister. Then she said, "It sounds and looks like it was quite a while."

"Um..." Sofie squirmed in her seat.

The truth was that Sofie was incredibly disappointed in her best friend. Or was it her *former* best friend?

Just about the same time that Sofie had moved back to Sweden, Jojo started spending time with Jessica – a classmate of theirs. She'd also started seeing Billy, a boy who lived on Sofie's old block.

During the Lindquist family's first few days in Sweden, Jojo had e-mailed frequently. And she'd written that she missed Sofie. But after a trip to Crete with Jessica, Jojo had pretty much stopped e-mailing.

At first, Sofie had been broken-hearted – and she was still very sad that their friendship didn't seem to be worth anything to Jojo. Sofie had really thought they'd stay friends, despite the distance.

Sometimes Sofie thought that Jojo's distancing herself might have something to do with Sofie's new interest in horses. They had always made fun of the girls in their class who rode horses in their spare time. Not in a mean way – and they'd never said anything to the girls – but both Jojo and Sofie had agreed that it seemed completely pointless to spend every free second at the stable.

Sofie didn't want to think that Jojo had ended their friendship just because Sofie had started liking horses. She'd thought about it, really tried to be honest with herself, and always reached the same conclusion: She'd *never* stop sending e-mails to Jojo just because her friend had a new interest. As long as that new interest wasn't illegal, anyway.

To like being with horses wasn't illegal, but Sofie still couldn't quite let go of the thought that maybe the horses were the reason for Jojo's silence.

Sometimes, especially if she woke up in the middle of the night, Sofie would think something terrible had happened to Jojo, and *that* was why she'd stopped writing to Sofie. What if she'd contracted an incurable disease, or been hit by a car? Still, Sofie knew that if something like that had happened, Jojo's parents would have told her. And they hadn't.

"She doesn't write a lot," she finally answered her sister.

"Oh?" Emma looked surprised. "Did something happen?"

Sofie stared down into her orange juice.

"Nothing, apart from me moving to Sweden and Jojo getting a boyfriend."

She didn't mention her thoughts about the horses. Maybe she was slightly worried that Emma would agree.

Emma looked sincerely sympathetic.

"That's too bad!" she said. "And mean... I think. I mean, it's not likely that you'll stay best friends forever – but you could at least stay in touch." She threw her hands out. "You were pretty much joined at the hip... like those... Siamese twins!"

Sofie sighed.

"I know. And now it's like we never knew each other."

It was good to get these things off her chest. Sofie hadn't told anyone about Jojo's lack of e-mails before. She'd always thought Jojo would change her mind. And by not talking about Jojo's betrayal, Sofie had tried to fool both herself and her family. It was somehow easier to pretend that nothing had happened if she didn't talk about it. Now she'd admitted to Emma that everything wasn't fine – and it was both a relief and a burden.

Sofie knew that Emma would tell their mother. Not because Emma was a tattletale, but because she probably thought it would be good if Elizabeth knew what was going on. Sofie also knew that this would lead to persistent attempts to fix everything.

Elizabeth believed that you could solve any problem by talking about it for hours and hours. This method did have its advantages, but Sofie didn't really want anyone else to get involved in what was going on between her and Jojo.

They should be able to fix their problems themselves. On the other hand, it might be good to get some advice.

"Have you confronted her?" Emma asked, taking a sip of her smoothie.

"How do you mean?" Sofie looked questioningly at her big sister.

"Have you written to her and asked why she stopped e-mailing? Have you told her you're sad because she stopped?"

"Not really..."

Sofie had, from the start, set her jaw and only sent happy, positive messages to Jojo. She'd been afraid to seem whiny and boring. Because who'd want to be friends with someone whiny and boring?

"Then I think you should," Emma said decisively. "If there's been some sort of miscommunication, you have to set it straight." She hooked a strand of dark hair behind her ear and looked her little sister in the eye. "How is Jojo supposed to understand that you miss her and that you're sad that you've lost contact if you don't tell her?"

Sofie sighed and shrugged.

"There is that..." She realized that Emma was right and decided to send an e-mail to Jojo that night.

"Jojo isn't a mind reader, is she?" Emma put the last piece of her sandwich in her mouth and chewed it. "Mmm... they have really good sandwiches here!" She wiped her hands on a striped napkin that matched the color of the wall behind them.

Sofie had barely touched her sandwich. And she didn't really feel like eating it. She felt like she had a big lump in her throat – a lump that grew when she thought of Jojo.

How could you just turn your back on eight years of

friendship? How could you forget your soul-twin after only a week? Had Jojo forgotten all the fun stuff they'd done together? Didn't she remember their slumber parties? Had she forgotten all the dance recitals they'd held for parents and siblings? Didn't she remember the secrets and the laughter they'd shared?

"Aren't you going to eat that?" Emma looked at her sister's half-eaten sandwich.

"No. I'm not hungry." Sofie drank the rest of her juice and pushed her tray to the side.

Emma raised an eyebrow but didn't say anything, and Sofie was grateful for it. If she opened her mouth to talk right now, she'd probably start crying instead.

Promising results

"Hi, Sofie! Did you have a good weekend?" Aunt Maggie, who always seemed incapable of standing still, greeted her niece happily as she leaned a pitchfork against the stable wall and got a running start with the wheelbarrow. It had to be emptied into the large container in front of the farm's garage.

"It was okay," Sofie answered and jumped to the side so as not to get hit when Aunt Maggie jogged up the ramp.

In the door to the little stable she met Tina, who was heading out with Rocky, a majestic, dark brown stallion.

"Hi!" Tina said. "I thought we should take Rocky and Champion out first today. Could you grab Champ? His head collar is on the hook next to his box." The blonde, shorthaired woman smiled at Sofie.

"Sure!" Sofie entered the stable and inhaled the sweet smell of horses and hay.

It was nice to be back at Humleby Farm after her weekend off. She liked the fast pace of the work there. Sofie rarely had time to think of other things, and right now, she wanted to avoid thinking about Jojo.

Sofie had been jealous of Emma this morning, since she

got to stay in bed and ignore the alarm clock when it went off at half past five. But now that she'd had breakfast and was in the stable, she felt much better.

She was met by welcoming neighs from a couple of the stalls and two curious horse heads appeared over the stall doors.

"Good morning, guys!" Sofie stretched her hand out to Champion's nose. His nostrils widened, and then he lightly nudged her hand.

"Sorry," Sofie said, patting his soft nose. "I don't have any carrots with me right now, but I'll make sure you get one later." She took the head collar, hanging next to the box as Tina had said, opened the stall door and sneaked inside with the brown gelding.

Sofie was still amazed that she could now dare go into a horse's stall – and even put on its head collar! It was such a cool feeling! She couldn't believe that she had become friends with these big, lovely animals! She'd always been so scared of them.

Okay, she only went into certain horses' stalls – the ones that were easiest to deal with. Still, Sofie was very pleased with herself, and she knew that Tina and the others were impressed by her progress. On her first day – just four weeks ago – she'd hardly dared to look at the horses.

Last week Sofie had even tried grooming a horse. She was doing better and better, even though she still jumped at unexpected noises and movements. She'd decided she wasn't going to give in to her fear.

A few times she had felt a strong sense of trust and understanding between herself and whichever horse she was working on. The feeling was hard to describe, but it was unbeatable, and she wanted to experience it again.

"Hello, Sofie!" Isabelle came rushing into the little stable with a lead rein in her hand. Sofie guessed it belonged to Oh My Gosh, the horse that had moved in when Speedy got placed in the same paddock as Sky. Isabelle had probably just let Oh My Gosh out in the paddock with Triple Tornado, another horse who spent his nights inside.

Humleby Farm consisted of four stables. Three of them were located in the same building complex, and were known among the staff as the "lower," "middle" and "high" stables. The fourth was located in the same building as the garage and for some reason was known as "the little stable," even though it was as big as the others. Sofie spent most of her time at the little stable, as did Tina, who belonged to the older group of grooms at Humleby Farm, and Sofie's cousin Isabelle.

In every stable there were eight to ten boxes, but half the horses spent the majority of their days outside. They were taken in each morning for care and training. Before the end of the workday, they were taken back to their paddocks.

Tina used to say that the outdoor horses had the most luxurious existence. They could move freely within the limits of the paddocks, they got to breathe fresh air for most of the day, and in the summer they had an unlimited grass supply.

Unfortunately, there weren't enough paddocks for all forty horses, but the ones who spent the evenings inside seemed to do just fine, and they got to spend a lot of time outdoors every day.

Sofie, who had never set foot inside a stable before coming to Humleby Farm, eventually learned that a professional trotting stable is quite different from other stables, for example, a riding school.

Almost all the horses at Humleby Farm were tenants of Uncle Tommy and Aunt Maggie. The horses' different owners paid Sofie's aunt and uncle for training and caring for them. That, in turn, meant that Uncle Tommy and Aunt Maggie didn't have complete control over which horses they worked with. If an owner was unsatisfied, or for some reason wanted another trainer, he or she simply moved the horse.

Sofie hoped with all her heart that the training and care that Humleby Farm provided would satisfy Speedy's owner enough to keep him there.

"Did you have a good weekend?" Sofie asked her cousin as she attached the lead rope to Champion's head collar and brought him into the passageway.

"Mostly work," Isabelle smiled and hung the lead on the hook next to Oh My Gosh's stall, "but if you have the best job in the world work isn't so bad. You?"

"Fine, thanks. Emma got here Friday night. We went to town on Saturday and spent yesterday on the beach."

Sofie thought she saw a flash of worry in her cousin's eyes when her sister was mentioned, but she hoped she had just imagined it.

"Sounds nice," Isabelle said. "Can you help Tina bring the horses from outside after you take Champ out? I'm going to get started in here."

"Sure!" Sofie said, going out in the yard with her brown friend. Saying good morning to Speedy was one of the highlights of her day.

"I'm excited to see how he does today!" Tina pulled her cap down to keep the sunlight out of her eyes.

Fredrik, who was an apprentice at Tommy and Aunt Maggie's, nodded.

"He'll be fine. He had some promising results last week."

Tina, Sofie, Fredrik and Josefin, one of the younger horse-keepers, were sitting on the bed of Humleby Farm's blue pickup, heading for the far paddocks. Roger, Humleby Farm's farrier and handyman, was driving the car. It was a nice, sunny morning, although very windy. The golden wheat in the fields beyond the paddocks billowed in the wind.

"You're talking about Speedy, right?" Sofie couldn't help asking.

"Yup, it's almost time for your honey to show us what he's got!" Fredrik smiled at Sofie. Everyone knew about Sofie's special feelings for the chestnut gelding, and she didn't mind.

She also didn't mind Fredrik. The apprentice with the dark, curly hair was always happy. He was a true animal lover, as well as a good driver. Sofie had thought, many times, that she could fall in love with someone like Fredrik, but he was seven years older than she was, so she decided not to think about it too much.

"I'm sure he'll do great!" Sofie smiled back. "Who's going to drive him today?"

"Probably me," Tina said. She turned toward Fredrik and shoved at him lightly. "Even though I know you really want to!"

"Oh, well... What's a royal ball?" He quoted the well-known line from Cinderella and sighed theatrically.

"Quit complaining! You're driving Lucia today," Tina pointed out cheerfully. "That's important too. Lucia has a race next week," she explained to Sofie. "It's her first since her knee injury."

"I know." Fredrik stretched. "And when I have my professional license I'm going to come back here and take Speedy Legend to unforeseen heights!"

"Hah! We'll see," Tina laughed.

Just then, they reached the paddock furthest from the stable, and Roger stopped the pickup so they could all pile off. When the truck bed was empty he did a quick U-turn and headed back to the farm in a cloud of dust.

"Someday, he's going to hit someone or something," Tina stated, following the dust cloud with her eyes.

Speedy and Sky were ready inside the fence when Tina and Sofie reached the paddock. The horses neighed softly, as if saying good morning to their keepers.

"Good morning to you too," Tina said, patting them both.

Sofie carefully walked up to Speedy and let him sniff her fingers for a few moments.

"Hi," she said softly. "How are you today?"

Speedy snorted and shook his head so that his blond mane flew in every direction.

"You don't like the wind either?" Sofie asked, patting him on the shoulder.

"Will you take Sky?" Tina had pulled up a plant that had wound around the fence and came walking with the strand, covered in pink flowers, in her hand. "They're pretty flowers," she said. "But that doesn't matter." Sofie nodded. An electrical fence had to be plant-free in order to work properly. She left Speedy and walked over to his dark brown friend. Sky met her eyes from underneath his long black forelock. Then he stretched his neck so he could sniff at her before she attached the lead rein to his head collar.

Sofie longed for the day when she'd be trusted to lead Speedy. So far, he was one of the horses whose stall Sofie didn't enter. And she couldn't lead him between the paddock and the stable either.

That was mostly because Speedy had been so unpredictable when he first arrived at Humleby Farm. Tommy and Tina had quickly decided that the then very nervous Speedy should whenever possible be cared for by only one person. Their tactic had worked well. After only a week or so, Isabelle, who was very experienced for her age, had been able to handle him as well.

Since Speedy had been very calm for the last few weeks, Sofie hoped that soon she'd be able to take care of her favorite as well.

Ten minutes later, they were all heading back to the farm. Sofie felt proud when she walked as one of the gang, with Sky on her right.

A stray thought of Jojo went through her head. For some reason, Sofie wished that her former best friend could see her now. She wasn't really sure why, but she guessed that she wanted to prove to Jojo somehow that it actually was fun to take care of horses. And that she could get by on her own, that she could have fun without Jojo.

That last part was only partly true. Sofie had fun without Jojo when she was working in the stables, but during her days off it just wasn't the same. Then she longed for someone her own age to share her thoughts with. The space that Jojo had left in Sofie's life couldn't be completely filled by Sofie's parents, Emma or Isabelle.

Every now and then, Elizabeth tried to convince Sofie that she'd probably get lots of new friends when school started in the fall, which wasn't much of a comfort. Sometimes, Sofie imagined that she'd end up as the victim of the class bullies – it was always easy to be mean to the new person.

"You won't be the only new person in class," Emma said when they were sitting on the bridge, chatting, that Sunday morning. "In the seventh grade there are usually at least a couple of new students. Sometimes they even split up two classes to make a new one. It'll be great!"

Sofie wasn't so sure. She dreaded the first day of school, and since Jojo hadn't kept in touch she was afraid that the London trip, which had been like a ray of light in the darkness, wouldn't happen. She didn't think she had anything to look forward to – except Speedy, of course.

Sofie heard the clopping of six pairs of hooves from far off. She quickly left her chores in the stable and went outside to meet the three horses and drivers as they entered the yard.

"Sixteen!" Tina called triumphantly from the seat of the long sulky behind Speedy.

Sofie gave her the thumbs-up sign and approached them. "Wow!"

Sofie had no idea what "sixteen" meant in this context, but she had no trouble understanding the look on Tina's face. Tina's smile spoke volumes.

Tommy, who had been at the course, supervising the training, came driving into the yard in the blue pickup. He parked and then hurried up to Tina and Speedy.

"That went well!" The trainer patted the sweaty chestnut and then turned to face Tina. "I'll call Axel and tell him the good news. In fact, I've registered Speedy for a qualifying race in two weeks. I think he's ready, but to be on the safe side I'm going to try to get him into a test race first. It'll have to be on Thursday."

Tina nodded.

"Makes sense."

"Yeah, I'd like to see how he'd behave on a bigger course, with more horses around."

"And you were right. Everyone in the business thought Speedy Legend was a finished chapter in the book of trotting history. Everyone except you and Axel."

Tommy nodded.

"Yes. I don't understand why everyone dismissed this horse so soon. He's only five; he's got years of racing ahead of him. But..." Sofie's uncle became silent for a moment and absently ran a hand through Speedy's blond mane. "You can't count your chickens before they're hatched. We'll have to wait and see how he does tomorrow, first of all. And then we'll have to look at how he does in the test race."

"I suppose." Tina signaled to Speedy to move forward, following the other two horses and their drivers. She turned around and called, "At least he's got speed in him! It felt really, really good today."

Tommy, who was already heading off to do chores, raised his hand to show that he'd heard her comment. Just like his wife, he seemed to have a hard time standing still and always seemed to be moving. Isabelle had complained to Sofie about it once.

"Sometimes, I wish dad had a real job. He's never free. Never! Not even on Christmas."

"My dad works Christmas sometimes too," Sofie pointed out. Stefan was a doctor, and it was partly because of the job offer he'd gotten from the Malmö city hospital that the family had moved back to Sweden.

32

"True. But he doesn't get up at five in the morning and work until half past eleven at night every day of the week, right?"

Sofie knew that Isabelle was exaggerating, but only a little. Running a trotting stable and, in addition to that, making training schedules for all the horses was more than a full-time job. The work also meant long trips to racetracks all over the country. Tommy often made round trips on race days, which meant that he had to leave really early in the morning and come home late at night.

"But you wouldn't want to live without the stables and all the horses, right?" Sofie asked her cousin. She knew Isabelle's dream was to become a catch-driver, a professional rider who usually didn't train horses, and drove other people's horses instead.

"No..." Isabelle had laughed. "You're right about that!"

News

There's nothing more depressing than an empty e-mail inbox, Sofie thought glumly, staring at her computer screen.

She'd e-mailed Jojo on Saturday night, as soon as she and Emma had come back from their shopping trip. The e-mail hadn't been as upbeat as the previous ones. Sofie had asked Jojo outright why she'd stopped writing. She'd even written a few lines about her liking horses and asked whether the silence had anything to do with that. She'd also come right out and asked if they were still friends, and if Jojo still wanted her to come visit before school started.

It was Tuesday, and there was still no answer from England. Sofie was beginning to regret being so honest. Maybe Jojo thought she was exaggerating? She imagined Jojo and Jessica taking turns reading the message aloud, laughing and trying to imitate her voice.

Jessica: "You and I were twin souls... That's *ridiculous*! She makes it sound like you were married or something."

Jojo: "Exactly. I don't see why she can't just let go and move on. She has to understand that we can't be best

34

friends when we live this far apart. I'm starting to feel like I have a stalker!"

Jessica: "She can stick to her horses."

Jojo: "Yeah, and you can't be friends with people who like horses. They smell!"

She was just imagining it, but Sofie couldn't help the sniffle that escaped her, sitting at her desk. Sometimes, life wasn't fair.

Just that morning Elizabeth had suggested that Sofie give Jojo a call, probably because Emma had told her that Jojo was no longer answering Sofie's e-mails.

"It's expensive to call someone in England, but since it's our fault that you can't see your best friend anymore, of course you can give her a call every now and then. As long as you tell us first." Elizabeth smiled encouragingly. "I should have mentioned that from the start."

But for some strange reason, Sofie didn't really want to call Jojo. Only a month had passed since they moved here, but to Sofie, it felt like more like a year. She'd been through so much in the past few weeks: the job at the stable, the fight with Isabelle, meeting Speedy... She hadn't been able to share any of it with Jojo. The North Sea lay between them like an ice-cold, insurmountable obstacle and seemed to be getting bigger and colder with each passing day.

Jojo was starting to seem like a stranger. Sofie could barely remember what she looked like. Well, of course she remembered that Jojo was blonde, had brown eyes and a dimple in her left cheek, but when she closed her eyes she could no longer see her friend's face clearly. It was as if the contours were blurring – as if she remembered the Jojo from her photo album, not the real Jojo. It was scary.

Riiiiiiing!

Sofie was awakened from her thoughts by the doorbell buzzing downstairs. Who could it be, visiting after 9 o'clock? Unexpected visits weren't exactly common in Humleby. No one could really say they were "just in the neighborhood."

Sofie wiped the tears with her shirtsleeve, left her room, and took a few steps down the stairs. Then she paused, trying to figure out whom Elizabeth was talking to down there.

Was it Aunt Maggie? Or Isabelle?

Yes, it was Isabelle! What did she want?

Sofie forgot that she was probably red-nosed and wet-eyed. She quickly ran down the stairs, and landed, both feet together, on the hall carpet.

"Hi! What are you doing here?"

Isabelle was still wearing her work clothes and it was obvious that Elizabeth had to keep herself from telling her not to go back outside.

Elizabeth didn't have many household rules. Sofie supposed it was because both she and Emma were pretty neat and orderly. But there was one new rule in their house: Never come inside with clothes that smell like a stable. Sofie couldn't understand why that was so important, but every mother had her quirks, she supposed.

"I have good news..." Sofie's older cousin answered, smiling secretively. She leaned against the doorjamb.

Sofie was instantly interested. Could it have something to do with Speedy?

"What?"

Isabelle straightened her blonde ponytail, looking as though she was enjoying the role of the messenger.

"You could say it's good news for both you and me..."

"Come on, Isabelle!" Sofie giggled. "Tell me!"

Elizabeth quickly suggested, "Why don't you take a walk? It's a beautiful summer night, and Sofie, you could use some fresh air after sitting in front of your computer all day."

Sofie was about to point out that she'd work outdoors all day, but decided against it. At the moment she was more interested in what Isabelle had to say.

The girls walked out onto the driveway of the Lindquist family's house. The gravel crunched beneath their sneakers and the noise made the neighbor's two horses lift their heads. They were always interested in the neighborhood happenings.

During her first weeks in Humleby, Sofie had thought it was horrible to live next to the big animals. They had been so close, and she felt as if they watched her whenever she was in the yard. Now, however, Sofie found it really pleasant to have two brown, hairy neighbors to talk to. The mares were both trotters, but they didn't belong to Humleby Farm. Their owner was a man named George. The horses were his hobby; he had a job as a janitor at a local school.

The two horses, named Lisa and Mrs. Brown, were sweet Thoroughbred trotters who liked company, and who always came up to the fence to say hi.

"Hi girls!" Sofie called to her four-legged neighbors.

Lisa neighed a reply and the horses curiously followed the girls with their eyes.

When they reached the village road, Sofie and Isabelle turned right and continued onto the less busy road – the one that the grooms used to get to the far paddocks.

"OK, now you have to tell me!" Sofie said as they passed the yellow house next to hers. She waved to one of the human neighbors' children, who was sitting on a tricycle on the other side of the low hedge.

"Okay." Isabelle slowed down a little. "Guess what's happening on Thursday?" Her eyes sparkled.

Sofie thought for a while, and then she said, "No idea."

Isabelle looked intense.

"Speedy is going to be in a test race!" she burst out, as if she were revealing some piece of important world news.

"But I already knew that," Sofie answered, disappointed.

Everybody at Humleby Farm knew that Speedy had been doing well, especially after Monday's training session. And Uncle Tommy had, that morning, announced that he was definitely going to Jägersro, the racetrack closest to the stable, for a test race on Thursday.

"You came here to tell me something I already know?" She looked questioningly at her cousin.

Isabelle seemed a little embarrassed.

"Well... Okay, let me put it this way: Guess who's driving Speedy in the test race?"

Sofie knew right away why Isabelle was so excited.

"Philip."

Isabelle turned toward Sofie, a big smile on her lips.

"Yes! Isn't it exciting!?"

Sofie nodded.

It actually *was* kind of exciting. The Philip Isabelle was talking about was one of the best trotting drivers in the entire country. He was a catch-driver, and in the last few years, he'd made his fortune on Sweden's trotting tracks.

Philip had been a trainee at Humleby Farm a few years ago, and he was a good friend of the Sandberg family. He sometimes stopped by before or after races at Jägersro, sometimes just to spend time with Tommy and Maggie, but sometimes to try out the horses Tommy particularly believed in.

Sofie imagined that Tommy was curious to hear what Philip had to say about Speedy. She also knew that Philip's opinion of Speedy wasn't what Isabelle found so exciting. Isabelle had a big old crush on Philip.

Not that Sofie could understand why. Philip seemed like a self-centered bore to her, and she also thought his looks were about average. He was too thin for her tastes, verging on scrawny.

Then there was the age thing. Isabelle was fifteen, and Philip was almost twenty-three! In Sofie's eyes, the famous driver was an old man. He also didn't seem all that interested in Isabelle.

Sofie hadn't mentioned any of this to her cousin. They didn't know each other well enough yet for her to share such confidences, and she didn't want to hurt Isabelle's feelings.

"Yes," Sofie answered. "Really exciting! When's he coming?"

"Tomorrow afternoon." Isabelle smiled. "I haven't seen Philip in a month. I've really missed him."

Sofie suspected that Philip hadn't missed Isabelle as much.

"Have you talked on the phone?" she asked.

"No, but you know... He's so busy. And I don't want to bother him. He's always very focused before his races and all..."

"He should still have a few free minutes every now and then, right?" Sofie pointed out, following the brown mare Leading Lady with her eyes. The girls had automatically turned onto the narrow gravel road that led between the paddocks and were heading toward the practice courses. Lady and her friend Star seemed to be playing tag. They'd been kept in a paddock closer to the stables previously, but they seemed to enjoy their new home just fine.

Isabelle shrugged.

"You don't have to talk every day just because you're almost going out."

"I suppose," Sofie answered. But she still found it odd that Philip and Isabelle didn't talk more often if they were, as Isabelle said, almost going out.

On the other hand, Sofie thought as they walked on down the hill, *I know nothing about love. Maybe I'd better keep quiet*.

Emma had had a couple of boyfriends in the last few years she'd lived at home, but they'd mostly waited by the door as Emma got ready to go out, so Sofie had never gotten a closer look at what going out with someone was like.

It suddenly hit her that maybe Emma was seeing someone right now. She would definitely investigate that mystery at some point.

"Oh, I can't wait until tomorrow afternoon ..." Isabelle sighed, dreamingly looking out over the paddocks.

"Mm," Sofie mumbled. She didn't really feel up to listening to more sighing and pining, so she turned off the gravel road.

Their walk had taken them all the way down to Speedy and Sky. The two horses were at the far end of the paddock, and Sofie started walking toward them quickly. Sky was standing a few feet from his friend, eating the juicy grass, just like Sky.

They looked up when they heard Sofie coming.

"Hi," she said. "How are you doing?"

"They couldn't be better," Isabelle answered. She'd caught up, and was now standing next to Sofie.

The wind, which had made bushes and small trees lie practically flat against the ground during the last few days, had finally calmed. A light breeze swept between the trees, and the leaves trembled. Other than that, everything was calm and still. The sun was low in the sky, but still warm.

The girls walked up to the fence and the horses came to say hi right away. They were probably hoping for a carrot, or maybe a slice of apple. They stood there, getting petted and scratched, for a long time, but then finally went back to their grass. Probably because they realized they wouldn't be getting any horse candy.

Sofie and Isabelle sat down next to the paddock, and stayed silent for quite a while.

Sofie guessed that Isabelle was daydreaming about Philip. She let her own thoughts flow freely. She felt a little better now than she had earlier in the evening. It had been tough, sitting by the computer, imagining Jojo and Jessica making fun of her.

And she was happy that Isabelle existed. They weren't best friends, but they *were* friends, and that was much better than having no friends at all.

Sofie liked Isabelle better with each passing day. Her older cousin wasn't as snobbish and ingratiating as she'd initially thought. If anything, Isabelle was a goal-oriented girl who wasn't afraid of hard work. The fact that she was very cute and made a doll-like first impression wasn't her fault. Isabelle only acted a little silly when Philip was around, or at least that's what Sofie thought.

Because of the great geographical distance between England and Sweden, Sofie's family had never really visited their relatives in Sweden much, but Sofie was already very comfortable in the Sandberg family's company. Uncle Tommy and her mom Elizabeth were brother and sister and had grown up together. And even though they were very different – like Isabelle and Sofie were, in many ways – there was an invisible bond that held them together. They had a history together.

"So, where's Emma tonight?" Isabelle was trying to sound casual, but Sofie could hear the strain in her voice.

"She's visiting a friend from elementary school, I think."

Emma had been in the fourth grade when the family moved from Sweden to London, and through the years she'd kept in touch with her best friend at the time, Lena. Sofie realized now what an achievement that was. Emma had made new friends – including a new best friend she was sharing an apartment with in London. But Lena had always been there, in the background. Sofie felt a pang of sadness when she thought about the fact that Jojo had already disappeared from her life, after only one month apart.

"Has she said anything about me?"

Sofie was jolted from her thoughts.

"What? Who?"

Isabelle looked questioningly at her younger cousin.

"Are you hard of hearing?"

"N-no, I was just thinking of something else." Sofie tried to shake off the sad thoughts that had been fluttering around in her brain moments before.

"I asked whether Emma's said anything about me."

"No..." Sofie thought for a while. "No," she repeated. "Nothing more than she thinks it'll be fun to get to see you."

"She said that?" Isabelle looked suspicious.

"Yes, she did."

"Hmm. Okay..."

Sofie got up.

"Forget all that old stuff. Emma doesn't even remember being mean to you when she was younger. She was just an annoying teenager then."

Isabelle smiled a crooked smile.

"Like you, you mean?"

"Yeah, or like you!" Sofie replied, pulling her cousin to her feet.

Just then they heard a rustling sound beyond the paddock. Sofie turned and saw two small boys among the trees. They started running when the girls spotted them.

"Hey!" Isabelle called after them. "What are you doing?"

The boys ran as fast as they could, toward the bigger road, without turning back.

"I'd really like to know what those two were up to!" Isabelle watched the boys run off.

Sofie shrugged. "Never mind them." She started walking toward the gravel road. "They were just kids, probably playing spies or something. Come on!"

Isabelle reluctantly followed her. She cast one last look at the boys, who were now far away.

"As long as they don't hurt the horses in any way."

"Why would they?" Sofie looked at her cousin, surprised. She couldn't understand why Isabelle was so upset.

"People can be very mean to animals," Isabelle answered, "usually because they don't know better..." She was silent for a long time, and then she said, "I saw something horrible once." She turned to Sofie, and her eyes were black with anger. "I was in elementary school and headed to shop class. I was alone for some reason... I was

43

just about to go through the door to the shop room when I saw some older guys on the soccer field. At first, I thought they were throwing a gray ball to each other, but when I looked closer I realized it was a *cat*! Can you imagine?" Isabelle gestured agitatedly with both her hands. "They were throwing the cat between them as if it were a ball!"

Sofie shook her head. What kind of person would want to hurt a poor, defenseless animal?

"What did you do?" she asked.

"I yelled at them, said that they were idiots and told them to put the cat down."

"That was brave."

Isabelle looked seriously at Sofie.

"It wasn't brave. It was a matter of life and death."

"Yeah... But they were older than you..."

"I didn't have time to think," Isabelle admitted. "I was so angry."

Sofie smiled.

"It's a good thing you were. Especially for the cat. How was it?"

"Fine, I think. It was a little shaken, but luckily, it hadn't been hurt." Isabelle turned toward the direction the two boys had disappeared. She muttered, "If those two boys get close to our horses again I'll..."

"Maybe they're just curious," Sofie suggested. "Maybe they *like* horses! All guys aren't cruel to animals... right?"

"No..." Isabelle calmed down somewhat. "I suppose you're right."

"Come on, before it's pitch-black out here!" Sofie urged her cousin on.

They hurried back toward the village and split up at the intersection outside Sofie's house.

"I'll see you tomorrow!" Isabelle called when she'd walked a few feet toward home.

Sofie waved and Isabelle waved back.

When Sofie checked her inbox again for the last time that day – and found it as empty as before – she was grateful for her newfound friendship with Isabelle. And the best part was, it seemed to go both ways!

The star driver arrives

"Okay, I think that's it for today." Tommy looked at the notice board above the dirty desk. "If there are no questions we'll get back to work," he said, turning toward the grooms.

It was Wednesday, and everyone was gathered for Humleby Farm's morning meeting. Every morning around seven the staff gathered in the middle stable to get information about which horses were going to be training, which ones were injured, and other things they needed to know.

The silence that followed Tommy's question showed that everyone had understood everything, and most of them started moving toward the door.

"When's Philip getting here?" Josefin asked when she passed Tommy on her way out.

Sofie saw Isabelle stiffen when she heard Josefin's question. She also saw Tina and Fredrik exchange significant glances, but she wasn't really sure what it meant.

Tommy looked at his watch.

"Well... sometime after two, I think."

"Okay." Josefin smiled and continued toward the door.

Isabelle, who had stopped at the yard, flew at Sofie as soon as she came out through the door.

"Why's Josefin interested in Philip?" she hissed angrily in Sofie's ear.

"She was just wondering when he'd get here." Sofie shrugged. "That isn't so bad, right?"

"She's always trying to impress Philip!"

So do you, Sofie thought, but she answered, "What do you mean?"

"Haven't you noticed?"

"No," Sofie answered sincerely.

"She always makes sure she's close to him!" Isabelle looked upset. "She's hangs around him like a child!"

Just like you, Sofie thought, smiling inwardly.

"I don't understand why she cares about him!" Isabelle continued. "He likes *me*."

"But then you don't need to worry, right?" Sofie pointed out.

Isabelle sighed.

"No, I guess you're right..."

The morning passed quickly. Lady and Star were each doing a quick practice test at the Jägersro track, and while Isabelle and Tina drove them Sofie mucked the mares' stalls. She also made sure there was new sweet-tasting silage for them when they got back.

Speedy was having a much-deserved day of rest. He was standing in his stall, looking like he wanted to get out of there. Sofie stood in front of the opening in the bars and talked to him for a while.

"Hi, Speedy Legend," she said. The chestnut came

47

up to her immediately. He stuck his head out into the passageway, sniffing at Sofie's outstretched hand. She looked around and found what he was looking for. "Look!" She bent down. "Here's a whole bag of candy."

Speedy stretched his neck, blowing air on the back of Sofie's neck. It tickled.

"Calm down!" she giggled, getting up. Then she broke a carrot in two and gave one piece to the eager horse. "Here you go!"

Speedy took the carrot and chewed it loudly. As soon as he'd swallowed the last piece he stretched his nose out to see if there was more.

"Oh, no," Sofie said sternly. "You can't stand here and eat a ton of comfort food just because you'd rather be out on the course. It's your turn tomorrow," she explained. "And it'll be Philip driving you."

The gelding neighed softly, as if to say, "Well, all right then."

When Sofie left the stable to head out to the bags of sawdust by the stable wall closest to the yard, she met Tina and Isabelle. They'd just passed the gates, and Sofie couldn't help smiling at the dusty sight.

It hadn't rained in over a week, so the ground was very dry. Tommy had watered the practice courses to keep the dust down so it wouldn't get in the horses' lungs, but the short stretch of the gravel road to and from practice had been enough to cover the long sulkies, harnesses, horses and drivers in gray dust.

"You'd both be perfect for a horror movie!" Sofie called to them. "*The Headless Horsemen* or something like that!"

Tina laughed and drove over the yard. Isabelle stopped Star by the bags of sawdust.

48

"I don't see anyone around on horseback," she said, smiling with dusty lips.

"Okay, *The Mystery of the Ghost Driver* – is that better?" Sofie wondered, parking her wheelbarrow in front of the bags.

Isabelle stuck her tongue out.

"Are you going to be the director, or what?" She signaled to Star to continue walking.

I'm glad it's dust and not mud, Sofie thought, looking at them. She had a feeling it was going to be her job to clean the horses and the equipment.

When Sofie got back to Humleby Farm after lunch, Isabelle was noticeably excited. Sofie noted that her older cousin had found the time to shower and put on some makeup during their lunch break.

"Hmm… is there a beauty pageant today?" Sofie teased. "Or aren't you going to work this afternoon?"

"I had to shower, you know," Isabelle answered. "The dust was itching."

"And you expect me to believe that?"

Isabelle giggled and Sofie burst out laughing.

Sofie liked teasing Isabelle. Now that they'd gotten to know each other a little better she noticed that her cousin actually had a sense of humor. And that she could take a lot of teasing before she got angry. It was nice that Sofie was finally able to relax and be herself around Isabelle.

Tina, who was standing at the far end of the passageway grooming Speedy, smiled when she heard the girls' laughter. She was happy they were finally getting along too. Sofie's first weeks at the stable hadn't been fun; not for any of them.

Tina never found out what the fight had been about, but she was glad that the girls had worked it out on their own. She was grateful that she hadn't needed to get Maggie or Tommy involved. Having to criticize her bosses' daughter wouldn't have been fun.

Tina liked Isabelle, who had only been ten years old when Tina came to Humleby Farm, and she thought the feeling was mutual.

Right from the start Isabelle had confided in the older woman on both big and small matters. And Tina had sometimes felt like an extra mother to Isabelle, whose parents were always busy. It was only recently that the teenage Miss Sandberg had become a little more closed off.

But Tina wasn't stupid, and she could figure a lot out on her own. She'd tried to warn Isabelle about Philip, but it wasn't easy to talk sense into someone who is blindly in love.

Maybe it's just as well that she learns from her mistakes, Tina thought, running the brush one last time over Speedy's chestnut coat.

Just then, there was the familiar sound of a car entering the yard.

"He's here!" Isabelle called excitedly. "Is it okay if I just run down there and meet him?" She looked pleadingly at Sofie. "I'll be right back, I promise!"

"Go," Sofie said.

Isabelle ran a hand through her hair, smoothed her T-shirt and then walked out onto the yard.

Tina, who was done with Speedy, shook her head but didn't say anything, and instead, turned to Sofie.

"What do you think? Should those of us who still have our feet on the ground take Sky and the two ladies out? I

50

suppose Philip will want to look at Speedy before we take him out to the paddock."

Sofie nodded.

"Should I take Sky?" she asked.

"Yeah, do that," Tina answered, leading Speedy into his stall. The gelding snorted, glaring at his keeper. He seemed annoyed because he couldn't go to the paddock right away. "Don't worry," Tina said, giving him some hay. "You *will* get to go out. Soon."

Sofie opened the door and entered Sky's stall. The sign next to the door said *Little Skywalker* and above it were two prize ribbons with *V-75* written on them. Sky had done well in his last few races.

"You're a good boy," she said, patting the gelding's neck. She put on his head collar and led the dark brown horse into the passageway. Then she fastened the crossties attached to the walls to his head collar and put a blanket on him, for protection against flies and the hot sun.

"Almost done!" Sofie attached the lead to the head collar and Sky shook his head, as if to make sure it was properly fastened.

Tina was waiting for Sofie, holding both Star and Lady. The mares had been showered and groomed after their training and were now eager to be out into the fresh air. Star nickered softly.

"I'm sorry, Star." Sofie looked around and met the mare's gaze. "I'm the slow one."

"You're doing great!" Tina gave Sofie an encouraging smile. "I have to admit I had my doubts on your first day... You seemed so afraid of the horses... And of me!" She winked at the last comment. "But you're tougher than you look!"

51

"To be honest, I *was* scared to death," Sofie admitted. "Well, not of you," she laughed, "but of the horses. And I wasn't all that interested either... But..." She nodded toward Sky. "There's something irresistible about these animals."

Tina nodded and said, "I agree completely!"

Sofie removed the crossties from Champion's head collar and hurried into the yard so that Tina could follow her.

Before they left the area Sofie had time to look toward the parking lot. She could see Isabelle and Philip standing by Philip's car, but Tommy was there as well and it looked like Philip was talking to him, and not his daughter. It didn't exactly appear to be a meeting of two people in love.

Happiness and cheating

When Sofie and Tina came back to the little stable it was almost half past two. They'd brought Oh My Gosh and Champion with them and now they tied the horses in the passageway. Isabelle was busy mucking out. She looked happy.

"How did it go?" Sofie wanted to know.

Isabelle blushed.

"Good!" she said, still energetically sweeping sawdust out of Champion's box.

"Is that all you've got to say?" Sofie wondered, going to grab a grooming kit.

"Shush!" Isabelle warned. "Philip will be here to look at Speedy any minute."

"But... Did it go well? Are you going to see each other again?"

Isabelle leaned her pitchfork against the wall and looked at Sofie, amused.

"You sound just like a curious little sister!" She put the wheelbarrow of old sawdust aside and brought one filled with fresh sawdust into the passageway.

"That's because I am," Sofie answered. She had started grooming Oh My Gosh. "But not yours, thank goodness!"

Isabelle grimaced in Sofie's direction.

Suddenly Fredrik stuck his head into the passageway.

"Hey, girls!" he called. "Anyone want anything from the gas station? I'm going to drive over and get an ice cream."

"Get me a soda!" Tina said. She was crouched down, putting hoof grease on Champion's hooves with a brush. "Orange, if they have it. Otherwise, anything's fine."

"Okay! Isabelle, Sofie, you want anything?"

Isabelle shook her head. "I'll go without today," she said.

"Get me a popsicle," Sofie asked. "Can you pay for it? I don't have any money with me."

"Of course, oh fair one!" Fredrik smiled, continuing toward the parking lot, whistling.

The staff at Humleby Farm had no organized coffee breaks; there was rarely time to sit down and take it easy. In the summer, they often had a soda or an ice cream whenever there was time and in the winter they sometimes went down to the gas station and bought hot chocolate or coffee, which they drank quickly.

There was a staff room in one of the barracks that belonged to the farm, and those who lived far away could eat lunch there, but leaving work just for a coffee break at a set time was difficult. You couldn't really leave a horse half-groomed or half-showered just because you were on break.

Just as Champion and Oh My Gosh had entered their cleaned stalls, Philip and Tommy appeared in the doorway.

Isabelle's cheeks flushed when she saw the famous driver.

"Hi!" she said eagerly. "Speedy's on the far right."

Philip nodded stiffly behind his sunglasses. The driver went into the stable with Tommy and then shook hands with Tina. Soon, they were all involved in a lively conversation about the chestnut trotter and his future.

Philip had passed Sofie without so much as even looking at her.

What a snob! she thought, annoyed, glaring at the thin guy dressed in a light pink shirt. *Would it kill him to say hello?*

Not that she really cared about him, but it was too bad that a good driver like Philip wasn't pleasant to be around off the track. She wondered if he was haughty to all young grooms.

Isabelle was standing behind the driver, as if she wanted to be part of the discussion as well, but no one took any notice of her.

Philip seemed, at least to Sofie, unusually disinterested for an almost-boyfriend, and she felt kind of sorry for her cousin.

He seemed much more interested in Speedy Legend. The driver entered the stall and inspected the horse from tip to tail while Tommy told him about Speedy's latest practice results. Philip seemed to like what he saw, and Sofie couldn't help but feel a little proud of Speedy.

Philip and Tommy were still standing outside Speedy's stall when Fredrik appeared at the door.

"Ice cream and soda!" he called, dangling a plastic bag in one hand.

Isabelle seemed to be permanently rooted behind Philip, but Tina excused herself and went to get her soda. Sofie got a popsicle.

"I'll go sit in the sun for a few minutes, if that's okay?" Sofie turned to Tina.

"Sure," the older groom answered. "We're pretty

much done here. We only have to take Speedy back to the paddock." She nodded toward Tommy and Philip. "As soon as those two chatterboxes are finished."

Sofie was just about to ask if she could take Speedy to the paddock when Tina continued, "You can lead him if you want."

There was a flutter in Sofie's belly and her face split into a grin that stretched from ear to ear.

"Really?" She almost didn't dare to believe what she'd just heard.

Tina laughed. "Yes, really. Would I kid you?"

"Thank you!" Sofie got to her feet and without thinking threw her arms around Tina's neck. "Thank you so much!"

"Whoa!" Tina exclaimed, somewhat surprised by Sofie's spontaneous expression of joy. She smiled and continued, "I'll go with you today, so we can see how it goes. But I'm sure it'll go well. Speedy likes it here now and he trusts us."

Finally! Sofie thought to herself when Tommy and Philip left the little stable fifteen minutes later. Now that she knew what was coming she could barely wait.

Before she entered the passageway she stopped, looking after the two men walking toward the Sandberg family's house. She had a feeling that Philip didn't want to be alone with Isabelle, because he never left Tommy's side.

"Congratulations!" Isabelle met Sofie in the passageway. "So the time has come, huh?"

"Yeah..." A nice warmth spread through Sofie's body when she caught sight of Speedy. He was so incredibly beautiful. His coat shone thanks to Tina's careful grooming and his intelligent eyes looked straight at her from beneath blond bangs. The white blaze and the four white socks were the chestnut's special distinguishing features. None of the other horses at Humleby Farm could hold a candle to her favorite.

Sofie smiled at Isabelle and Tina.

"Can I put on his head collar?" she asked.

"Give it a shot!" Tina said. "He shouldn't be any more difficult than Sky."

Sofie took the head collar from the hook next to Speedy's stall and entered with a pounding heart. Speedy lifted his head and sidestepped a little in the sawdust.

"Hey buddy," she said softly, letting the horse sniff at her for a few seconds. Then she put on the head collar.

Isabelle gave a long whistle behind her.

"I never would've thought, a few weeks ago!"

Sofie attached the lead and proudly led Speedy into the passageway.

"Me neither!" she laughed.

Tina and Isabelle followed Sofie and Speedy into the daylight.

"I'll tag along if that's okay," Isabelle said.

"Of course," Sofie answered. "But I thought you had other things to do." She winked at her cousin.

Isabelle shrugged.

"Philip and Dad have a lot to talk about. I'll see him at dinner tonight."

Sofie walked, straight-backed, with Speedy on her right. She could feel the heat from the big animal and she loved every second of it.

"This is going well, right?" she whispered to the gelding and patted his shoulder carefully.

Speedy walked on calmly. He seemed to be completely at ease with the fact that it wasn't Tina or Isabelle walking next to him. Sofie realized that she and the beautiful trotter had more than one thing in common. They were both new at the farm and they both had big challenges ahead of them.

Speedy was about to show everyone that he was still as fast as he was a year ago, when he'd won the Swedish Trotting Derby and been considered one of the best trotters in Sweden.

Sofie was going to prove that she could take care of her favorite horse. She was hoping she'd get to help out at Humleby Farm after school started in the fall as well. Afternoons and weekends wouldn't be a problem. Maybe she'd even get to go along as a groom when Speedy had an important race at some point in the future? A wonderful mixture of nervousness and anticipation spread through her body.

Sofie had borrowed some of Isabelle's books about horses and one about trotting. She read a little from them every night but kept them under her bed because she didn't want her father to see them.

Sofie still found it annoying that Stefan had been right about her attitude toward horses. On the day that he'd got his objecting daughter the job at Humleby Farm, he'd told her that she'd one day learn to like the four-legged animals – and Sofie had stubbornly disagreed.

But Stefan had been right. And even if Sofie had revealed through her actions that she didn't mind going to the stable anymore, she definitely didn't want to be discovered reading books about horses in her spare time!

At home, and especially in front of her dad, Sofie made it look like she was happy with her job, but nothing more. She actually thought it was really exciting to read about horses *and* to be with them.

But, Sofie thought, a small cloud temporarily obscuring her view of the sun, *it's a pity that all these fun things are happening at the expense of my friendship with Jojo*. She really wished she could tell Jojo about Speedy and her job. It would've been even more fun if she could.

The group rounded the stable and went out onto the gravel road that ran behind the barracks and past the paddocks closest to the farm. The narrow road was a perfect shortcut to the far paddocks, but they only traveled it on foot or on horseback.

Suddenly Isabelle stopped with a gasp.

"What's wrong?" Sofie stretched to try to see what her cousin had seen, but Speedy was in her way.

Without a sound Isabelle turned on her heel and ran back toward the stable.

"Isabelle!" Tina called, but the girl had already rounded the corner of the house.

Sofie stopped and turned to ask Tina what was going on. To her big surprise she saw her older colleague put a finger to her lips.

"Shh!" she said.

Sofie shook her head, confused, but Tina gestured for Sofie to keep going, so she urged Speedy to walk.

Just as the gelding started walking again, Sofie saw something pink close to the barracks, behind Speedy. She quickly bent down, peeking out under the horse's neck.

And then she could see clearly what Isabelle must have seen. In the shade of the big oak tree was Philip in his pink shirt, but he wasn't alone. Josefin was standing close to him. And they didn't seem to be talking about the weather. They *couldn't* be talking – since their lips were pressed together in what seemed to be an eternal kiss!

61

Back to square one

"Brrr!" Sofie shivered and raised her eyes toward the threatening clouds that were stacking up above the stable rooftops. She turned around and gloomily confirmed that it looked equally dark in all directions.

How weird, Sofie thought as she walked along the village road, *yesterday was ice cream weather and now I'm cold*. She hoped for Speedy's sake that it wouldn't start raining, but it didn't look as if there was much hope of that. To be on the safe side she'd brought rubber boots to work that morning. She carried them in a plastic bag in her left hand, while writing a text message to Jojo with her right thumb.

Up until now, Sofie had only e-mailed her friend in England, mostly because that was the cheapest method of communicating. She had to pay half her cell phone bill herself, and she knew it was extra expensive to call and send text messages internationally.

Maybe she'd also chosen not to send any texts because a message like that was so revealing. You could always blame an unanswered e-mail on computer troubles, but cell phones were rarely broken. Sofie knew that Jojo always had her phone with her – and that if she didn't answer a text message it was because she didn't want to. *That* she decided not to do.

Sofie suspected that right now Jojo was busy sending romantic texts to Billy and secret messages to Jessica, but she didn't want to go on imagining anymore. She wanted answers. If Jojo wanted to end their friendship, she might as well know now. No more beating around the bush.

Sofie wondered if it was the weather that was making her moody this morning. Nothing out of the ordinary had happened, so that might explain why she felt extra sad. Her e-mail inbox was still echoingly empty. She still hadn't heard anything from Jojo.

Hi! Why don't you get back to me? Miss you. // Sofie

Bzzz. The message whisked away through space, and should already be in Jojo's phone, ready to be read. But would she answer?

Sofie passed the high gates to the stable area and continued toward the little stable. She waved to Roger who was jogging toward the lower stable and he waved back. A chilly gust of wind swept over the yard and made gravel and dust whirl around Sofie's feet. Then she felt the first drop of rain hit her nose.

"Typical," she muttered, thinking of Speedy. Soon he would be transported to the track for his test race – why did it have to rain today?

Sofie wished with all her heart that she could've gone to see the race, but she knew that wasn't possible. Tina and Tommy were taking Speedy to the race, and Sofie and Isabelle had to stay behind and take care of the horses in the little stable.

63

❀ ❀ ❀ ❀

Isabelle was another story. After the incident with Philip and Josefin the day before, Isabelle had disappeared and was nowhere to be found. Tina had muttered something about the fact that Philip probably had "a girlfriend in every trotting stable in southern Sweden," and added that she'd tried to warn Isabelle.

Sofie, who had doubted Philip's feelings for Isabelle all along, was in one way happy that the driver had been caught red handed. She'd never liked him, and she disliked him even more now. She hoped Isabelle would find a more suitable object for her affections.

Still, Sofie felt bad for her cousin, because even if Isabelle was the only person who thought Philip liked her more than as a friend, it had been her reality. Isabelle had interpreted Philip's short comments as declarations of love, and feeling let down must have been awful. *That* was something Sofie knew all too well.

Quite a few times that Wednesday evening Sofie had set out toward the Sandbergs' house to check on Isabelle, but she'd changed her mind and turned back every time. She wasn't really sure what she was going to say to her cousin. She knew nothing about boys and love!

Sofie had thought that it would probably seem ridiculous if she, an inexperienced thirteen-year-old, tried to comfort someone who was fifteen. She guessed that maybe Isabelle had probably dated a lot of guys. So she had stayed home.

Sofie also felt she didn't know Isabelle well enough to go find her when she was sad. It was one thing to tease her older cousin in the stable, but being there for her when she felt bad seemed much more difficult.

Sofie hoped that Isabelle had managed to get out of bed on this gray Thursday, because she didn't think she'd be able to take care of eight horses by herself – including the hard-to-handle Rocky Road.

As if to confirm that thought, when she entered the little stable she was met by three calm horses, dozing in their stalls, and one angry stallion – who was chewing the bars on his stall doors even though the hatch was open.

"That's stupid, Rocky!" Sofie berated the dark brown horse. "Where's that going to get you?"

Rocky glared at her, flattened his ears against his head, and continued chewing on the iron bar.

"You should be neutered," Sofie stated. "Then you'd be able to think of something other than the fact that you are a big, beautiful stallion. And then you'd probably get even better track results." She shrugged her shoulders in resignation. "At least, that's what Tina says."

Rocky Road was one of the most charming horses at Humleby Farm, but also one of the most impossible to deal with. Tommy wanted to neuter the horse, since he thought Rocky would benefit from it. But the horse's owner was of a different opinion, so there wasn't anything Tommy could do about it.

Tina, Tommy and Isabelle were pretty much the only people who could handle the unpredictable stallion. Sofie would never dare enter Rocky Road's stall. When she was close to him, she felt about as scared as she had her first day at the stable.

To her great relief, Sofie noticed Isabelle standing in the shadows at the far end of the passageway. She walked up to her cousin, unsure of what to say.

"Hi..." she started. "How are you?"

65

Isabelle, who hadn't heard Sofie enter, jumped at Sofie's voice and then turned to face her younger cousin.

"I've been better," she answered, pushing a strand of blonde hair from her face. Her gaze shifted to Speedy, whom someone had already brought in from the paddock. Sofie looked at the beautiful chestnut gelding as well.

"I get that..."

Sofie hesitated. What was she supposed to say to comfort Isabelle? Maybe listing Philip's bad character traits right now wouldn't be too smart?

Sofie really felt like saying there were probably a lot of people who were nicer and more fun than the famous driver, but she checked herself. She suspected Isabelle wasn't receptive to information like that right now.

"Are you very sad?" she asked at last.

Isabelle smiled crookedly. Her eyes were red-rimmed, and she didn't look like she'd slept a lot during the night.

"Hmm. Yes... Sad... and angry. I'm angry with Philip and Josefin, but mostly, I'm angry with myself. For thinking there was something between us. And... because I still like him..." The last sentence was swallowed by a choked sniffle and a tear slowly rolled down Isabelle's cheek.

"You still like him!?" Sofie looked at her cousin, surprised. "How can you like him after what happened yesterday?" She regretted her words the second they left her mouth. She realized they sounded harsh.

Isabelle turned around quickly and glared at Sofie.

"I've liked Philip for years!" she snapped. "It's not something you can shut off just like flipping a switch!"

Isabelle turned on her heel and stomped out of the stable.

"B-but the horses!" Sofie called. "I'm sorry, Isabelle! Come back!"

Sofie felt the feelings she'd had the first time she'd come to the stable bursting to the surface. There was a rush of fear in her belly.

Would everything become that horrible again? Would Isabelle start ignoring her or throwing mean comments at her all the time – just because Sofie had managed to put her foot in her mouth? Was their newfound friendship really that fragile?

It seemed like she'd have to take care of all the horses in the little stable by herself. Devastated, she saw herself being dragged behind Rocky Road as the stallion trotted over the wheat fields at record speed.

For a few moments, Sofie considered talking to Aunt Maggie, but she realized that would just be embarrassing. What was she supposed to say to her aunt? That Isabelle had boy trouble and was angry because Sofie had said something stupid?

Then suddenly Isabelle was standing in the door with a pile of clean blankets in her arms.

"Let's get the horses out," she said flatly without looking Sofie in the eyes. She gave Sofie Champion's blanket.

The girls worked silently the entire morning. Sofie had a dull ache in the pit of her stomach. She glanced over at Isabelle every now and then, hoping that their eyes would meet and everything would be like it used to. But the older cousin seemed very concentrated on her chores. She didn't look in Sofie's direction even once.

Tina came to work soon after Isabelle and Sofie had left the little stable together with Rocky Road and Champion. The girls' older colleague noticed right away

67

that something was wrong, but she didn't have time to ask what was going on. There were lots of things that needed to be taken care of before Speedy's test race and she spent the majority of the morning running back and forth between the stable and the horse trailer.

Just after nine o'clock Speedy nobly walked up the ramp, ready for the short trip to the racetrack. He seemed very calm and collected. The rain had stopped, and the yard was no longer dusty. Now it was sticky instead.

Sofie abandoned her chores for a few minutes and wished her favorite horse good luck.

"Run like the wind, boy!" she said just before Tommy slammed the door behind Speedy, "but don't gallop!"

"No, no such silliness," her uncle smiled, getting into the car. "I'll see you around lunchtime! Keep your fingers crossed that the weather doesn't get worse," he said through the open driver's side window. Then he started the engine and drove out through the gates.

Tina waved from the passenger seat and Sofie gave her the thumbs up. Then she walked back toward the little stable. There, more work and an angry Isabelle would be waiting for her. Yippee...

When it was five minutes past twelve, Sofie parked the feed cart at the far end of the passageway and stretched.

"I'm going home to eat," she said. "The horses have been fed. I put some protein food in Speedy's crib too. He's going to be hungry when he comes back, right?"

Isabelle, who still hadn't said a word since their conversation that morning, nodded without taking her eyes off the harness she was greasing.

Sofie sighed and walked out onto the yard. She knew that

Isabelle had been hurt by her comment, but she thought her cousin was overreacting. Also, Sofie had said she was sorry, and she was pretty sure Isabelle had heard her apology. So Sofie thought it was Isabelle's turn to be a little magnanimous. But maybe it wasn't all that easy to be magnanimous when you'd just been passed over for a dark-haired beauty like Josefin?

Just as Sofie walked out onto the village road there was a beep in her pants pocket.

A text message! From Jojo?

Hands trembling, Sofie fished her phone out of her jeans pocket and opened the message.

Hi Sof! I'm kind of stressed out. I'll talk to you later. Jojo.

Sofie had to stop and read the text again. "I'm kind of stressed out"!? Was that all she could say after almost a month of silence?

Dejected, Sofie stared at the display, trying to analyze the reply. Was there anything to read between the lines? Did Jojo seem angry?

No, Sofie thought sadly. Jojo isn't angry, she's indifferent. She doesn't even seem to understand I'm serious! Had her friend in England even read the long e-mail Sofie had sent her on Saturday night?

Sofie put the phone back in her pocket and walked on heavily. She had almost decided even before she read the message, but now, the decision was definite. She was not going to go visit Jojo in London in August. What was the point in going there when Jojo was ignoring her?

The worst part was that Isabelle had stopped talking to her too. She was back to square one. She had no one! The lump in her throat that she'd felt on Saturday was suddenly back again, and it seemed bigger this time. The tears burned behind her eyelids.

Sofie was so occupied with her own thoughts that she didn't hear someone calling her name at first.

"Sofie!"

She turned around and spotted a familiar horse trailer that had stopped at the intersection by the Lindquists' house. Tommy was leaning out through the open window of the car.

"Hi there!" He smiled widely. "You seemed to be daydreaming."

"Hello," Sofie struggled to achieve a smile. "How did it go?" she managed to get out.

"Awesome!" Tommy told her proudly. "Speedy Legend is a name to count on. He was the first one across the finish line! And he had a really good time, too."

"That's great!" Sofie swallowed hard to keep the tears away. Her voice didn't really carry. She hoped she wasn't going to start crying right in front of her uncle.

"By the way, Aunt Maggie wants to invite your family for dinner tomorrow night," Tommy continued. "Could you ask your mom if that's okay?"

Sofie nodded.

"Okay, I'll ask her," she said.

An angry driver honked at the horse transport, which was blocking traffic on the little village road.

"I'd better move on," Tommy said. "I'll see you later!" He turned back out on the road and then continued toward Humleby Farm. From the corner of her eye, Sofie saw Tina turn around, looking worriedly at her. The concern in Tina's brown eyes was just the thing to make her tear ducts flood. The salty tears rolled down her cheeks. Drip, drop.

Sofie felt a sting of guilt, since she couldn't even be happy about Speedy's success.

Crisis meeting

With her head hanging, Sofie walked up the driveway toward the red brick house. She was completely unaware of the fact that her every step was registered by two pairs of dark eyes on the other side of the hedge. Lisa and Mrs. Brown were standing silently underneath the big chestnut tree, somewhat disappointed about not getting any attention. The two mares had gotten used to the dark-haired girl talking to them as she went past.

Sofie opened the gate in the low wall between the house and the old garage. She closed it after herself and took, without looking, a big leap up the stairs to the kitchen door. Halfway through her leap she noticed that something was in the way.

On the top step, Emma was sitting with a neon green iPod on her lap. On the next step below her, she'd placed a bottle of nail polish, a bottle of acetone and a bag of cotton balls. She was painting her nails a light pink color and humming along to a song. It sounded horrible.

If Sofie had been in a good mood, she would've torn the

headphones off her big sister's ears and mimicked her off-key singing, but right now, she just wanted to sneak past without being seen.

Sofie's wish was destroyed the moment the thought went through her mind. Emma, who had seemed completely absorbed by the music, quickly grabbed Sofie's pant leg and held her there.

"Stop!" she said, removing the earphones. "What happened? You look terrible."

Sofie wondered if her sister had some kind of sixth sense, or maybe eyes in her forehead, because she had no idea how Emma had been able to spot her – and notice that something was wrong – in half a second.

Sofie's first instinct was to run past her sister and lock herself in the bathroom – forever. But for some reason she didn't. Instead, she did something unexpected; she told Emma everything. She told her about Philip and about Isabelle's silence. She revealed that Jojo hadn't replied to her latest e-mail and showed Emma the text message.

"I wish we'd never moved back to Sweden!" Sofie sobbed at the conclusion of her long monologue. "I want everything to be the way it used to! I want to live in London, I want a best friend, and I want to be in a class where I know everyone!"

"Okay, I understand." Emma offered Sofie a clean cotton ball to wipe her eyes. "I haven't got anything else," she said apologetically, "but it should work." She waved her hands in the air to dry her nail polish.

Sofie accepted the cotton ball, still sobbing, and wiped her eyes as best she could. Emma stopped waving her hands, moved the bottles, and pulled Sofie down on the stairs next to her.

"Let me tell you something," she said, looking her little sister straight in the eyes.

Sofie looked away, waiting to hear a long lecture about staying happy, and being strong and open to new impressions. (Sofie had realized that her sister was getting more like her mother with each passing day.)

But instead, Emma said, "Do you have any memories of what it was like when we moved to London?"

"Uh..." Sofie thought for a few seconds. "No, not really," she answered. "I was only three years old."

"Precisely," Emma said, nodding, "but I was ten and I remember it very well."

Sofie suddenly saw her sister in a new light. She'd never thought of that before – that maybe Emma hadn't wanted to move to London, that maybe Emma had been as sad then as Sofie was now.

"I had been in the same class for four years," Emma said. "Well, five if you count kindergarten. And suddenly, I was supposed to start over. I didn't know a single person when I entered the classroom the first day in fifth grade. It was awful. I just wanted to go back to Sweden, to my old class and to Lena. I hated Mom and Dad because they'd decided that we were moving. I thought the worst part was the fact that they never asked me. They just decided everything."

Sofie nodded. She'd felt exactly the same way when Stefan and Elizabeth had told her that they were moving back to Sweden. Why had they never talked about this before?

"How long did it take you to adjust? When did you stop feeling homesick?"

Emma tucked her knees under her chin, looking out at

the yard. The neighbor's orange cat walked past on the lawn, not paying the magpies in the birch tree any attention, even though they were screeching threateningly. A butterfly fluttered around above Elizabeth's newly planted lavender.

"I think I wanted to go home for almost a year." Emma looked at her little sister again. "I cried myself to sleep many nights. Back then, it wasn't all that common to have your own computer or Internet at home, so Lena and I wrote each other regular letters. It took days for a letter to get where it was going, and I remember thinking the wait was unbearable. The letters from Lena were what got me through the first few months. She always wrote long letters. I've saved them all."

"Having your own computer and an Internet connection isn't much good if your friend doesn't reply to the e-mails you send," Sofie sobbed.

"True," Emma answered. "But listen: what I really wanted to say was that most of us have to go through something hard at some point in life. But pretty much every time something good comes from the mess sooner or later. In hindsight, I'm happy we moved to London. If we'd stayed in Sweden, I never would've learned English so well, I'd never have met Linda and all my other friends in London, and I wouldn't be able to say I feel at home in two places in the world."

"But..." Sofie thought for a while. "If you'd stayed you wouldn't have had to cry yourself to sleep for an entire year – and I'm sure you'd have gotten just as many good friends here. And also, that's easy for you to say *now*. If someone had asked you back then –"

"I would've said I wanted to go back," Emma filled in, "of course." She put a hand on her little sister's shoulder and said, "I *understand* you think it's awful right now, but it'll get better. It will. I promise."

"I can't think of one single good thing that's happened since we got here..." Sofie sniffled, her eyes filling with tears again. "Jojo's ignoring me, Isabelle is angry all the time and..."

"You're forgetting something." Emma looked sternly at her.

"What?"

"If we hadn't moved, you'd still be afraid of horses," her big sister stated simply. She got up decisively.

"Now we're going to eat mom's delicious pasta salad with ham and cheese. And then I'm coming with you to the stable."

Sofie blinked the tears from her eyes and looked at her sister, surprised.

"W-what?"

"I said, I'm coming with you to the stable." Emma put her hands on her hips and continued, "There's not much we can do about Jojo. She's in England, and she's apparently forgotten how a real friend is supposed to act. But Isabelle is close by, so we'll have to deal with her instead."

"No!" Sofie exclaimed, shocked, and jumped to her feet. "You can't!"

Emma looked at her little sister, annoyed.

"Why not?" she wondered. "Don't you want me to help you?"

"Yes. Yes, I do, but..." Sofie hesitated. Should she tell Emma what Isabelle had said about her? Maybe she'd get angry, and that wouldn't be a good base for a reconciliatory talk.

"Spill it! I can tell there's something you haven't told me."

Once again Sofie had the feeling that her sister had a

sixth sense. She already felt so exhausted by everything that had happened that morning that she didn't really feel like talking, but Emma looked so commanding. And she did want help.

"Okay, okay... But can we eat first?" The thought of her mother's pasta salad had rekindled her appetite, and there was only half an hour left of her lunch break.

"Sure." Emma herded Sofie through the kitchen door.

"Wait, I have to take my shoes off outside," Sofie said, walking back out on the stairs. "You know what Mom thinks..."

Emma rolled her eyes.

"Oh, I know," she said, laughing. "Shouldn't you take off your shirt and your jeans too?"

"No time," was the answer.

Sofie kicked off her sneakers on the sunny stairs and hurried after her sister into the house. On her way to the kitchen, Sofie realized she had a feeling of anticipation about the afternoon. She was very nervous about what would happen when Emma and Isabelle came face to face, especially considering the state Isabelle was in. But the knowledge that she'd get to show her workplace to her big sister meant she could live with having to confront her cousin.

Sofie had looked forward to showing Emma what the stable was like and getting an opportunity to show off a little with her new skills. It was fun to know something her big sister knew absolutely nothing about for once.

Emma steps in

"Hi, Sofie!" Tina came out of the little stable and brightened when she saw the Lindquist sisters. She extended her hand. "You must be Emma." She smiled. "I'm Tina, a colleague of your little sister," she explained.

"Hi!" Emma shook hands with the blonde woman. "Nice meeting you. I've heard a lot about you."

"And?" Tina winked at Sofie. "I hope all good things."

Emma laughed. "Only good things, cross my heart!"

"Great! I'm sure Sofie will want to show you around a little before she starts her chores." Tina turned to Sofie. "Give your sister a tour and we'll start when you're done. I'll be right back."

"Okay!" Sofie smiled thankfully at Tina. "Come on, Emma! I'll show you Speedy!"

"I've already seen him many times," her sister pointed out. "But sure… you can show him to me again."

They continued along the passageway and Sofie eagerly told Emma about the horses as they passed them.

"This is Sky," she said, pointing to the dark brown gelding. "He goes in the same paddock as Speedy. The brown mare without a star is Leading Lady and the horse with the white star on her forehead is Divine Star. Isn't she lovely?"

"Well…" Emma shrugged, "I guess."

Sofie laughed.

"You really are hopeless! But I won't yell at you. I would have answered the same way myself a few months ago."

Finally, they reached Speedy's stall.

"Ta da!" Sofie made a flourish like a circus manager introducing the next act. "The amaaazing… Speeedy Legeeend!" She turned to her sister. "Did I tell you he ran a test race today? I met Tommy afterwards and he –"

Sofie interrupted herself in mid-sentence. She realized that somebody was standing at the far end of the passageway, staring at them. And that somebody was Isabelle. In her eagerness to show the stable, Sofie had forgotten her cousin and all the bad things that had happened earlier during the day.

Emma, who still hadn't seen Isabelle, gave her little sister a surprised look.

"What is it?" she asked. "Did a bumblebee fly into your mouth, or something?"

Sofie squirmed. "Well… no…"

At that moment, Emma discovered Isabelle. The older girl didn't hesitate for a second, but went right up to her cousin and hugged her.

"Isabelle, hi!" she exclaimed. "Long time no see!"

Isabelle looked as if she wanted to run away.

"H-hi," she stammered.

For a moment, the silence was deafening. The only sound was the trampling and chewing of the four horses, and Sofie nervously waited for the big quarrel to explode.

Emma broke the silence.

"You remember me, don't you?" she asked Isabelle.

"Yes. Yeah, sure…" The blonde girl answered slowly.

"Great!" Emma cheerfully said. "It's been a while…
When was it, really? Hmm…" She pretended to think.
"Three years ago, maybe?"

"Well… I guess," Isabelle whispered. She seemed to be
scared out of her wits of Emma. It looked as if she expected
her older cousin to eat her alive, or maybe worse.

Emma smiled.

"Sofie says you're really good at taking care of the
horses here."

Isabelle looked down. "Oh… well…"

"Yes, really," Emma insisted. "She says that you and
Tina are fantastic."

Isabelle opened her mouth as if she wanted to say
something, but Emma went on.

"Personally, I'm pretty scared of horses, to tell the truth.
I really admire anybody who dares get close to them." She
laughed. "You're brave!"

Sofie gave her big sister a surprised look. Had Emma
gone with her to the stable just to say the things about
Isabelle that Sofie had never said? Had she come here to
butter up their cousin? Sofie had thought that Emma was
planning to put Isabelle in her place and tell her how to
treat other human beings.

Isabelle looked up and met Emma's eyes again.

"Horses are kind animals." She quickly smiled. "You
have to be loving but firm. Just like when you bring up a
dog – or a child, I guess."

"Sounds right." Emma nodded thoughtfully. Then she
went on, "Can't you come along and show me the other

80

stables? I'm pretty sure you know more than Sofie about the other horses."

"Well… yeah… if you want…" Isabelle was uncertain.

"Absolutely!"

Sofie glared at her sister but only got a mischievous smile in return. Emma winked at her and gestured for her to come along.

Sofie shook her head. Emma didn't give a hoot about horses. Why did she want Isabelle to tell her about them? Sofie didn't understand, but she still followed the older girls when they walked out into the yard and headed for the upper stable. Maybe Emma was planning an elaborate "smack down" of their cousin and didn't want to risk Tina being around?

At first, Isabelle was somewhat aloof, but as they proceeded she seemed to relax more and more. By the end, she was eagerly telling Emma about the different horses and their quirks.

Sofie, who at first had been sulking behind the other two, finally, reluctantly, had to admit that her sister had actually accomplished something important: she had broken the ice. And furthermore, this seemed to be the sole purpose of the guided tour. A "smack down" didn't seem to be part of Emma's plan.

Isabelle seemed to enjoy being a guide and Sofie couldn't help listening to what she said. Her older cousin was a good storyteller and many of the small anecdotes they heard were pretty funny.

On their way back to the little stable, they met Aunt Maggie. The energetic woman immediately threw her arms around Emma and started asking lots of questions. Emma was happy to see her aunt, and the two were soon deep in conversation.

81

Sofie wasn't sure what to do. Should she go back and help Tina? Or should she say something to Isabelle? Her cousin didn't seem angry anymore, so maybe this would be a good time to say something?

"I'm sorry."

Sofie jumped at the unexpected words.

"What?"

"I'm sorry," Isabelle repeated. She had moved a little closer to her younger cousin. "I acted like an idiot earlier today."

"Well, yeah," Sofie said. "I guess you overreacted a little... But that's all right. I know that you're sad."

Now, when Isabelle was in a good mood again, it felt unnecessary to hold a grudge.

"Yes, but that's no excuse for acting badly."

Sofie shrugged. "It's OK, really. I'm glad that you said you're sorry."

"Great!" Isabelle quickly hugged her younger cousin. "I like you. You're not just 'my little cousin in England' anymore." She smiled. "You are a real friend."

Sofie felt happiness run through her entire body. Imagine, Isabelle actually regarded her as a friend! That meant she had at least one friend in the world...

At the same time, she was a little embarrassed. What would she say?

Sofie didn't want to seem too happy – that could make Isabelle think that she'd never had a friend before in her life. But she still wanted to say that she was glad for what Isabelle had said. It was hard to find the right words.

"Thanks. Or... same to you. I..."

"Did you ask your mom if you can come to dinner tomorrow?" Aunt Maggie saved Sofie from continuing her embarrassing speech and Sofie was relieved, but a few seconds later she realized what Aunt Maggie had said.

"Oh!" Her face was hot. "I forgot!"

Aunt Maggie shook her head but smiled.

"Kids today… What's in your head, exactly?"

"A lot of *important* things!" her daughter explained.

"Ha, ha!" Aunt Maggie laughed loud and heartily. "I think I'd better call Elizabeth instead. That seems more reliable." She quickly glanced at her watch. "Oh!" she exclaimed. "I have to run to meet a sports reporter. He's writing a big article about somebody you know…" She smiled mysteriously.

The three girls gave her curious looks.

"Is he going to write about Philip?" Sofie said. Philip was in the sports pages regularly.

Isabelle looked down and Sofie bit her tongue.

"Nope. Not this time," Aunt Maggie said.

"Is he going to write about Dad?" Isabelle asked. To Sofie's great relief, she seemed to have decided to forget that Philip's name had been mentioned.

"No, not your father either." Aunt Maggie laughed. "Last guess," she said, "and then I have to run."

"Is it Speedy?" Emma asked, and Sofie looked at her sister with surprise. What did she know about Humleby Farm?

"Right!" Aunt Maggie exclaimed. "It seems they're dedicating a whole page to Speedy's comeback, with nice big pictures…"

"He hasn't raced yet," Isabelle said, "except for the test race."

"I know." Aunt Maggie shook her head. "That's exactly what your dad said when the journalist called. But he was persistent, that guy. He said he'd seen Speedy at the track this morning and wanted to be first with the news."

At that moment a red car turned into the yard.

"And here he is," Maggie said, hurrying toward the car. She gestured to the driver to park along the fence.

The girls walked back to the little stable. They really had to start working now.

"That's so exciting!" Sofie said when they walked into the passageway. "It's going to be great to read about Speedy in the paper. I hope they take some really nice pictures!" She turned to her cousin. "Do you think it's possible to order copies from the photographer?"

"Well, maybe." Isabelle was thoughtful. "If all this doesn't put too much pressure on him. If everybody thinks he's going to win…"

"No problem," Sofie said, with a smile on her lips.

Isabelle raised her eyebrows in surprise.

"How can you be so sure?" she carefully asked. "I mean, don't get me wrong, but…"

"Don't you see?" Sofie's eyes were sparkling with laughter as she looked at the older girls. Suddenly, she lost control and couldn't get a single word out. Instead, she folded up and giggled wildly, almost falling over.

Sky neighed anxiously in his box and Emma and Isabelle gave each other questioning looks. Emma shrugged.

"I guess it has something to do with her age," she said to Isabelle, "or maybe she's sick."

The comment made Sofie snort and giggle even more. Tears started running down her face and laughter spilled out of her. Emma and Isabelle's confused faces didn't help either. They looked so funny!

For a moment, Sofie wondered if she actually was sick.

Maybe she even was going crazy? Just a moment ago, she had been angry and sad – and now she was laughing like a loon.

A second later, she realized that it was normal to laugh. It was just a shock, since she hadn't laughed like this since she left England. This thought helped her to collect herself enough to say, "I mean, really… How's Speedy supposed to feel pressure about being in the paper?" She giggled again. "Does he actually *read* the paper?"

They were silent for half a second, and then both Emma and Isabelle broke out laughing. A minute later, all three were giggling as wildly and out of control as Sofie had been.

Sofie enjoyed herself. She found it unbelievably freeing to lose control and just let her laughter gush out. She never wanted that feeling of happiness to end. After a few minutes Emma said, "You know what, Sofie?" She was out of breath.

Sofie shook her head, gasping for air. She couldn't say a single word.

"Sometimes, you're actually pretty funny!"

Isabelle collapsed into a small giggling heap in the passageway.

"Thank you," Sofie huffed to her sister.

"But just sometimes! Remember that," Emma reminded her, trying to look serious.

Sofie's stomach cramped up and she had to lean on her big sister to keep from falling over. "Help!" she squealed.

"Never," Emma grinned, wiping her tears with her hand. "It's your own fault!"

Tina came out from Star's stall, glanced at them with amusement and was glad to see that everybody was in a better mood.

"Okay guys, the fun's over," she joked. "We have work to do!"

The decision is revealed

"What were you thinking?" Sofie kicked a pebble that bounced on the uneven pavement.

"When?" Emma watched the pebble.

"Yesterday, when we met Isabelle," Sofie explained, kicking another pebble. It flew away and landed on Tom's lawn. Tom was a widower who lived in the little house across from Humleby Farm.

"Be careful, or the old guy might come running out and tell you off," Emma cautioned.

"He wouldn't dare when Dad's here," Sofie calmly said. She nodded in Stefan's direction.

"Oh, he's one of *those*." Sofie knew very well what Emma meant.

Tom was a grumpy old man who didn't mind telling lots of people off. But for some reason, he had a great deal of respect for Stefan. He even seemed just a little afraid of him.

Several times, Emma and Sofie had noticed grownups looking up to their dad. Stefan had explained that it probably was because certain professions were regarded as "better" than others in the past. He mentioned doctor, teacher and priest as examples.

Tom actually seemed to believe that their dad was a little better and a little finer than other people, since he always bowed and took his cap off when Stefan passed by. Sofie really couldn't understand how anybody could worship her dad. Stefan was just an ordinary human being. And sometimes pretty irritating.

But the strangest thing about Tom was that he didn't even say hello to Elizabeth. He didn't seem to keep women in high regard.

Sofie had just started wondering how Tom would have acted toward her mother if Elizabeth, too, had been a doctor, when her sister interrupted her.

"Well…" Emma said, returning to Sofie's question about yesterday's meeting with Isabelle. "The second best trick to get people to relax is to praise them. That's why I buttered her up a little."

"Isabelle *is* good with horses," Sofie said as they crossed the road and walked up the driveway to the Sandberg's house. "But I never said that she's 'fantastic.'"

"I know," Emma said cheerfully. "But a white lie is never a bad thing, if it makes people feel better."

"So which one is the best trick?" Sofie wanted to know. "You said praise is the second best."

"Right." Emma smiled. "The very *best* thing you can do is to show your own weakness, to reveal something that you're bad at. Or afraid of."

Sofie immediately understood.

"So saying that you're afraid of horses was also a part of your plan?"

"Yes." Emma looked satisfied. "Isabelle relaxed

immediately when she realized that I wasn't trying to outdo her in any way."

"Yes, right... She actually did," Sofie mused. "But are you really afraid of horses? I didn't know that."

"I'm not afraid, but I'm not all that interested either." Emma grinned a lopsided grin. "And I don't feel totally at ease around them."

Sofie realized that her sister, who in many ways could be totally obnoxious, was actually quite smart about understanding other peoples' feelings. She made a mental note to remember the tricks Emma just had taught her. They might come in handy someday.

"Welcome!" Aunt Maggie was suddenly standing at the stairs. "How good to see you!" She hugged each and every one of them. "Daniel is home, too," she said, turning to Emma. "I thought it might be fun for you to see him."

"Great!" Emma said, smiling.

Sofie knew that Emma, just like herself, wasn't too fond of Isabelle's big brother. He acted like a snob and always talked about how well he was doing at the university. But as Sofie had just discovered, Emma was a social genius, so maybe Emma would manage to get him to relax a little.

"I set the table on the enclosed porch today," Aunt Maggie said, showing them into the house. "They say it's going to rain tonight so we're better of with a roof," she explained.

"Great," Elisabeth smiled. "The air has been a lot cooler since it rained yesterday, so picnicking on the lawn doesn't sound all that nice."

"We can always open the doors if it gets hot on the porch," Maggie suggested. "Please have a seat, ladies and gentlemen! The food is ready."

89

The dinner turned out to be nicer than Sofie had expected. She sat at one end of the table with Emma, Isabelle and Daniel. As she had guessed, Emma was able to lure unexpected (i.e. nice) traits from her older cousin, and several times Sofie found herself laughing at Daniel's jokes.

While they all stuffed themselves with Aunt Maggie's tasty food, the conversation bounced back and forth over the table like a tennis ball. In most discussions, both children and adults took part with lots of energy.

Sofie really liked Tommy and Maggie. They always listened to what you said and treated everybody the same, regardless of age. She suspected that Isabelle wouldn't really agree with her – but that probably had to do with their being her parents. Your own parents don't always seem to treat you with the respect you deserve…

Through the half-open door of the enclosed porch, Sofie could see out across the beautiful garden and the pastures beyond it. She suddenly felt very happy. Here she was, sitting with a bunch of people she loved, surrounded by green pastures and beautiful horses. Looking between two pink geraniums, she could see Lucia and one of her horse pals from the upper stable running across their paddock, playing tag. It looked wonderful. A fleeting thought of Jojo passed by, but Sofie managed to brush it away. Tonight, she wanted to be in a good mood.

"So, did you see the paper today?" Tommy threw the question out and everybody at the table nodded eagerly.

Sofie smiled. "I ran to the mailbox as soon as I woke up!" she said.

"So what did you think of the article?" her uncle asked.

"It was great. Wonderful! But…"

"Was anything missing?" Tommy gave her a surprised look.

"No, no," Sofie quickly said. "It's just that it felt like I was reading about… well, a fairytale horse. I didn't really recognize the real Speedy."

Tommy nodded.

"Well, you know, journalists… They always lay it on thick." He smiled. "But then, it's their job to write in an interesting way, to make us want to read what they're writing."

"Of course," Sofie nodded, "but all that about Speedy being 'ready for slaughter' when Axel bought him, maybe that was just a little *too* thick?" She made a face. She had hated that part of the story.

"It was exaggerated," Tommy answered, "you're right. Speedy wasn't in good shape when he came here, but he wasn't totally out of it."

"Wasn't he?" Aunt Maggie entered the conversation. "I think most people thought that Speedy Legend was a falling star."

"Many thought that he wouldn't be able to keep up with the best," Tommy explained, "but I think quite a few others could see a future for Speedy at a lower level."

"The pictures were amazing, by the way," Elizabeth said. "From those photos, you might actually believe that he really is a fairytale horse. That one of him against the light was really beautiful, a work of art."

Everyone agreed, and they kept talking about the newspaper article and the chestnut horse for a long while. Even Emma, who wasn't really interested in horses or trotting, entered the conversation of hope and expectations.

"It would be fun to see the qualifying races," she said to her uncle. "Do you think I could sneak in through the back door?"

"Absolutely!" Tommy smiled at his niece. "Just tell me how many tickets you want, and I'll get them for you."

"Thanks! Great!"

Sofie felt jealousy pricking at her. She wanted nothing more than to go with Speedy to the track and see the race. Actually, she would have done almost anything to be there. But there were seven other horses to care for – and they couldn't be forgotten just because Speedy was in a qualifying race. Tina was Speedy's keeper, and she was the one who would go with him and prepare him for the race.

Isabelle leaned over and whispered in Sofie's ear, "How about us offering to feed the horses? My rear end is starting to feel sore." She smiled.

"I'd love to." Sofie didn't mind using her legs for a while. And she certainly didn't mind seeing her four-legged friends in the stable.

"Thanks for the food, Mom." Isabelle got up. "Sofie and I'll feed the horses now."

Sofie also got up.

"Thanks, Aunt Maggie! It tasted wonderful."

"Thank you, girls." Maggie smiled at them. "And it's great of you to take care of the horses. We'll have dessert on the table when you get back."

"What's for dessert?" Isabelle asked.

"Ice cream with home-made hot fudge," her mom answered.

"Yummy!" Isabelle pulled at Sofie's sleeve. "Come on, if we hurry we won't have to help clear the table!"

Sofie closed the door to the Sandberg's house and inhaled the fresh evening air. It was still light outside, but the sun was low. A swarm of gnats was dancing in the shadow of the apple tree closest to the house.

"Mmm. Just a month ago, I had no idea that fresh air could be this lovely!"

Sofie filled her lungs with another deep breath while they rounded the corner of the stable and came into the yard.

"Sometimes you say these really weird things." Isabelle gave her younger cousin a skeptical look.

"It's not weird at all," Sofie defended herself. "In London, the air was never this clean. Not even if you were out in the garden at night."

"I wouldn't imagine that the air is very clean here either." Isabelle got the wheelbarrow and started walking for the bale of silage. "But it might be cleaner than in London… I never thought about that before."

"You'd think about it if you went there." Sofie dragged out a bale and laboriously got it into the wheelbarrow. Isabelle tore open the white plastic with a key, and together they spread the silage in the cart.

"It would have been fun to go to London…" Isabelle said while turning the hay cart and pushing it up toward the little stable. "I wonder why we never went to see you while you lived there."

"Probably because your parents can never take more than one afternoon off," Sofie pointed out.

"I guess you're right…" Isabelle sighed a little and pushed the cart into the passageway.

They were met by snorts and soft neighing from the four stalls that were occupied right now. Rocky put his magnificent head out above the stall door to see who was visiting. The dark brown stallion seemed to like what he saw.

"Time for your evening snack!" Isabelle yelled and was immediately met by enthusiastic neighing.

Sofie opened Champion's stall and threw some silage on the floor. Mentioning London had reminded her of Jojo, and she suddenly felt a knot in her stomach. As much as she tried, she couldn't forget that Jojo still hadn't answered her e-mail. And she couldn't accept the indifferent text message that she had gotten in response to her simple, but very seriously meant, question: *Why don't you write me?*

Her decision not to go to London in August still felt completely right – in view of how Jojo was treating her. But it still hurt. How could Jojo just ignore her? They had been best friends for more than eight years!

"By now, I think you've earned money for that flight to London!"

The Lindquists were walking home after the dinner with their relatives. It was almost midnight and darkness had settled over Humleby. Stefan put his arm around his youngest daughter and cheerfully went on, "I can help you book the ticket on the Internet if you like. That's often less expensive."

Sofie pressed her jaws tightly together. She could feel Emma's eyes boring into her neck, and she knew that sooner or later she would have to tell the truth.

"I'm not going."

"What?" Stefan suddenly stopped, grabbed Sofie's shoulders and turned her around. "What did you say?"

Sofie looked down at her sneakers. The streetlight gave them a strange color.

"I'm not going," she repeated quietly.

Stefan was confused. He looked at Elizabeth, who shook her head to signal that she hadn't known anything about this. Emma shrugged her shoulders and pretended to have no idea what Sofie was talking about.

"What happened?" Stefan looked at Sofie with worry in his eyes. "I thought that the trip to London was very important to you!"

Sofie squirmed. She knew that this would lead to detailed interviews and offers of solving the conflict. But how could her parents help when even she herself didn't know what the problem was? She definitely didn't want them to call Jojo's parents and start digging for what happened – that would only make everything worse.

"Can't you at least answer my question?" Stefan asked her. "What happened, Sofie and why haven't you said anything?"

"Nothing's happened." Sofie could feel that she was going to cry soon. She swallowed and went on, "It's just that Jojo doesn't seem to care anymore. I haven't heard from her for days…"

"B-but… What's that supposed to mean? I thought you were e-mailing each other all day long. I can call Simon if you want…"

Simon was Jojo's dad and also a former colleague of Stefan's.

"No!" Sofie looked at her dad with horror in her eyes. "Don't drag him into this." She tried to smile. "It's cool, Dad. I just don't want to go."

"Well, all right…" Stefan shrugged. "It's your decision.

If you don't want to go, you don't have to. But it's too bad… You and Joanna have been friends for so long."

"Come on, darling." Elizabeth hooked her arm into Stefan's, and the family started walking again. "It'll be better to talk about this tomorrow. It's late now, and you always see things different in the daylight."

Sofie blinked away a tear. She knew that nothing would make her change her mind about the trip to London.

Jojo had made her decision for her.

An explanation

It had been almost impossible for Sofie to fall asleep when she came home from dinner with the Sandbergs on Friday night. In a way, it felt good to have dropped the bomb – sooner or later, she would have had to tell her parents that she wasn't going to London. But she knew that as soon as she got out of bed her mother would start dissecting the problem until she knew every little detail. Elizabeth had this strange ability to get people to talk even if they didn't want to.

In the wee hours, when Sofie finally managed to sleep, she was thrown back and forth between strange dreams. In one of them, she was pursued by an enormous chestnut horse with enormous fangs. Jojo was in front of her, but she couldn't reach her. In another dream, she was sitting on the floor, tearing Isabelle's horse books to pieces. Sofie had been all sweaty when she woke up. She had to look under the bed to make sure the books were still there, and that they weren't damaged.

As usual, Sofie booted the computer when she got up. She had finally stopped hoping for an e-mail from Jojo –

and now that Emma was here, she didn't send any e-mails either. But you never know... The last thing to go is hope.

When the computer signaled that there was an unread message in the inbox, Sofie's first thought was that it was of the usual spam. But still, her heart started beating faster. She clicked the message open with a shaky hand.

From: Joanna Nilsson ‹jojo_sweetie@britmail.com›
Date: Sunday, July 20, 2008 9:32 a.m.
To: Sofie Lindquist ‹sofiesofine@swedemail.com›
Subject: Sorry!!!

Hi, Sofie!

I know – I've been acting like a jerk. I guess you won't want to see me ever again... but I still want to try to explain:

When I heard you were moving I was so depressed. It was always you and me against the world! I knew how lonely I was going to be. We'd always had each other and we hadn't cared too much for the other girls in our class.

When I ran into Jessica and Louise outside the store that day at the beginning of the summer, it felt as if I had to hold on to them. Just to have <u>somebody.</u>

At first, both Jessica and Louise were very nice to me. They seemed to feel sorry for me because you'd moved away. And that felt good, of course.

So when Jessica asked me to come with her to Crete, I said yes, because it seemed better to go there with her than to sit at home with Mum and Dad all summer.

When we were in Crete, Jessica suddenly started saying a lot of nasty things about Louise – and I chimed in, because I thought maybe Jessica and I could be together in school this fall. I saw a chance not to be lonely.

But I NEVER meant to desert you. I always thought that we'd stay best friends even at this long distance.

The problem with Jessica is that she wants to do EVERYTHING together – like, you know, go to the bathroom and so on… She's been more or less glued to me all summer (except when I saw Billy) and I haven't had even a minute to send e-mails or text messages. And even worse, Jessica didn't like me e-mailing you! I think it made her jealous somehow.

You must think that all this sounds really weird, like some kind of phony excuse, but it's actually the truth. I wanted so much to fit in with Jessica, since I was scared to death of being alone.

At the beginning of the summer, Jessica said that she thought my clothes were dorky, and that I should use more makeup. I went straight out and bought a bunch of designer clothes and makeup (my dad went crazy!) just to satisfy her. It seems totally wacky now when I think back on it! I'm really ashamed to admit it.

Last week, it felt as if she and I were friends for real. But just the other day, we got into a fight about some petty matter, and it ended with Jessica going home. Yesterday, she sent me a text message, saying that she and Louise were friends again, and that they didn't want to see me again.

It's just now that I can finally see what a creep Jessica really is. She just takes and takes, but never gives anything back. I even broke up with Billy for her sake!!!! (She thought he was too childish for me.)

It's as if I've been hypnotized and just woke up. I can't understand how I could just ignore both you and Billy! I like Billy and YOU are my best friend. It's YOU I should have stuck to.

*I can understand if you hate me, but of course I hope
that you can forgive me. I wish all this had never happened.
Miss you a lot!*
Hugs,
Jojo

Sofie rubbed her eyes and stared at the screen. She read the
message three times, and she didn't know what to think.
One part of her wanted to just swallow the whole thing
in one gulp, make up with Jojo and hope that everything
would be like before. But on the other hand, she couldn't
really buy Jojo's explanation.

First of all, it seemed unbelievable that Jojo wouldn't
have had a single minute to send an e-mail or a text
message. Nobody can be that busy! And secondly, Jojo had
her free will and could think for herself. Had she really
been totally brainwashed by Jessica? This sounded weird
and very unlike Jojo.

"Sofiiie! Breakfast is ready!" Elizabeth called from the
kitchen.

"Coming!" Sofie got into a pair of sweatpants as she
read the last lines of Jojo's e-mail one more time.

*I can understand if you hate me, but of course I hope
that you can forgive me. I wish all this had never happened.
Miss you a lot!*

Jojo certainly seemed regretful. But could Sofie really
trust her? What if it turned out that the real problem was the
horses? Would Sofie then have to choose? And what would
actually happen if Jessica came around again?

With her head full of questions, Sofie went downstairs to
have breakfast.

Bread, ham, cheese, and muesli were on the table, but

100

the chairs were empty. It seemed the rest of the family had taken their breakfast outside. By a quick glance through the window, Sofie confirmed that the sun was shining in a clear blue sky. She decided to follow suit, although she didn't really want to be with her parents right now. What she really didn't want was to continue the discussion that had begun on their way home from Humleby Farm. Also, the situation had changed a lot by now. After reading Jojo's e-mail this morning, Sofie wasn't at all as certain about her decision as she had been the night before. Right now, she didn't want to talk about the trip at all. She needed time to think.

The sharp light blinded Sofie when she stepped out on the sun-warmed concrete. She elegantly balanced a bowlful of yogurt and muesli in one hand and a plate with two sandwiches, towering on top of a glass of juice, in the other.

"Wow! How much are you going to eat?" Emma looked up from the funny pages in the morning paper.

"I'm hungry," Sofie announced, sitting next to her sister.

"I can see that…"

Stefan and Elizabeth were at the fence, chatting with the neighbor, and Sofie was relieved when she realized it would be a few minutes before Elizabeth's interrogation could begin.

"I…" Sofie began, immediately biting her tongue. Should she really tell Emma about the e-mail?

"What?" Emma gave her little sister a questioning look. "What did you say?"

"Oh, nothing." Sofie took a big bite from her sandwich so she wouldn't have to speak for a while.

"I'm sure it was." Emma didn't give up. "Did Jojo answer yet?"

Sofie stopped chewing, looking at her sister in disbelief. Then she swallowed and said, "Did you read my e-mail?"

"No, why should I? I brought my own laptop."

Sofie took another bite from her sandwich.

"So you did get an answer?" Emma went on.

"Yes." Sofie washed down the sandwich with some juice. "It came this morning."

"And, what did she say?" Emma looked curiously at Sofie. Emma loved to analyze what people said and didn't say, and she seemed to have some talent for character judgment. Still, Sofie felt that she wanted to form her own opinion first.

"I'll tell you later."

Emma opened her mouth to say something, but Sofie held up her right hand.

"I said I'll tell you later."

Emma closed her mouth and with some disappointment went back to *Calvin and Hobbes*.

Sofie looked out at their well-tended yard. The raspberry bushes stood in straight lines, with narrow paved walks in between. In the flowerbeds, new little plants were arranged by height and flowering season. In the past few weeks, her parents had put up trellises and planted different kinds of climbing vines.

They had done a great job cleaning out weeds and cutting bushes since they came to Humleby. And what's more, they seemed to think it was fun. Sofie couldn't understand how anybody could have a real interest in birdbaths or perennials, but it was nice that her parents had found a hobby that they could share. They seemed to be enjoying life more than ever, which was fun – for them.

Sofie let her eyes wander from the garden to the big

birch trees in front of the horses' barn and suddenly decided to greet the neighbor's horses. She left her plate and glass on the table and walked barefoot across the soft lawn and toward the hedge.

Behind the thick foliage was the barn where Lisa and Mrs. Brown lived. The barn went all the way along the west side of the yard, meaning that the horses had plenty of room. There was a gate in the middle of the hedge. Sofie used this shortcut but was careful not to step in the poison ivy that grew thick next to the fence.

The two brown mares immediately noticed Sofie when she was standing by the fence, and trotted up to her from the other side of the barn. Both of them stretched their necks across the fence to smell their visitor.

"Hi," Sofie said, letting Mrs. Brown examine her fingers with her soft muzzle. "I guess I've been forgetting about you for the last few days…"

"Iiihaaahaaa!" Lisa agreed, lightly pushing at Sofie's arm.

"I'm sorry." Sofie smiled and patted Lisa's neck. "I've had a lot to think about, you see. Isabelle and I had a falling out again… because of that stuck-up Philip…" She thought for a moment and then went on. "We're friends again now. Thanks to Emma, actually. But this morning I had an e-mail from Jojo. She says she's sorry, but I really don't know… What do you think?"

Mrs. Brown bent down to graze in the juicy grass, but Lisa stayed where she was, looking at Sofie with her dark eyes.

"Iiihaaahaaa!" answered Lisa.

Sofie laughed.

"I wish I could understand what you're saying, because I'm sure it's very wise."

103

There was a noise down by the fence at the crossroads and both horses turned to see what was happening. When they realized it was George coming with hay, they hurried over to him.

Sofie waved to the old man, who raised his hand and waved back. He threw out some hay for his horses and then walked up to her.

"Hi, Sofie!" George smiled until his eyes almost disappeared behind all his wrinkles of laughter. "I see you're back, talking to my ladies."

"Yes…" Sofie was still thinking about Jojo and didn't realize that she had a worried wrinkle between her eyes.

"You don't look too happy today." George watched the brown-haired girl. "Is something wrong?"

Sofie surprised herself with her honest answer. "My best friend in England has ignored me all summer," she explained, "and now she wrote to say she's sorry…"

"Well, that's good, isn't it…?" George smiled again.

"Well…" Sofie mused. "I'm not sure I can trust her after what happened…"

"Pah!" George straightened. He put one hand at the small of his back and made a face, as if he had a backache. "You shouldn't hold grudges," he went on. "Believe me, life is too short for that. Why don't you just call her? Often, you can tell from people's voices what's going on."

"Maybe…" Sofie smiled at the old man. "Thanks for the tip, anyway!"

"Not at all." George laughed a little. "Just let me know if you want me to fix any more problems for you." He patted Lisa, who had run back along the fence with Mrs. Brown.

The old man waved goodbye and started for the stable,

but before he left the paddock he turned and called out, "See you!"

"Yes, see you!"

Sofie returned to the garden, collected the things she had left on the table and went into the kitchen.

Her mom was there, cutting rhubarb into small pieces. Sofie could feel that the Great Moment of Questioning was dangerously close. Nobody else was in the room and she knew Elizabeth would jump at the chance.

"Good morning, dear." Elizabeth smiled at her daughter. "Did you sleep well?"

"Oh yes," Sofie assured her." She nodded at the pile of rhubarb. "Are we having rhubarb pie for dessert today?"

"I invited the neighbors for coffee this afternoon," her mom explained, still working with the knife.

"Okay." Sofie quickly put her plate and glass into the dishwasher. Then, before Elizabeth had the time to start her interrogation, she hurried to say, "Mom…"

"Yes?" Elizabeth had started measuring the ingredients for the pie pastry. She cut a thick slice of margarine and put it in a bowl, but when her daughter didn't continue, she looked up, meeting Sofie's eyes.

"Is it…" Sofie swallowed. "Is it okay if I call Jojo today?" she said.

Misgivings

Every morning, the whole week after the phone call, Sofie actually jumped out of bed when her alarm went off. Then she walked to Humleby Farm with quick, easy steps. It didn't matter if the sun was shining or if the weather was more like a wet and windy October day – Sofie still felt as if she were floating above the ground. For the first time since her family moved back to Sweden, she felt at peace with life in every way.

The phone call to Jojo on Saturday was, of course, one important reason for Sofie's good mood. She had been so nervous. Yes, it had actually been *scary* to dial the well-known number to the Nilsson's, and after two rings she had been close to hanging up.

Yet she had composed herself. Somewhere inside, she was sure that George was right. The chat with the old man had worked a little like an alarm clock for Sofie. She had realized that there actually was no reason to walk around feeling sad all summer – supposing that Jojo really meant what she wrote in her letter.

It had been a great relief to hear Jojo's voice on the

phone, and after a somewhat stiff beginning, it almost felt as if they had never left each other.

Jojo had assured her, over and over again, that she was ashamed and that she had acted like a fool.

Finally, Sofie heard herself say, "It's okay, Jojo. You're forgiven."

"R-really?"

"Yes…" Sofie mused for a few seconds before going on, "You can't do more than say you're sorry, can you? And I know how terrible it is not to be forgiven." She had thought about how Isabelle had ignored her after her comment about Philip the week before.

"Thank you…" Jojo sounded touched. "Thanks, *darling* Sofie! I feel a lot better already."

They talked for more than forty minutes, after which Elizabeth started drawing closer to the sofa where Sofie sat. Sofie understood what she meant and ended the conversation with the words, "Mom seems to want me to hang up now, but… It was fun talking to you, Jojo. Good to hear your voice again."

"Yours too," Jojo answered. "I promise to e-mail you soon. Cross my heart. And by the way…"

"Yes?"

"Do you still want to come and see me before school starts?"

Sofie hesitated for a moment, but then said, "Yes… Yes, I guess I do… Let's talk next week, okay?"

"Okay."

When Sofie hung up, she was soaring. It had been such an unbelievable relief to talk through everything with Jojo. And George had definitely hit the nail on the head. As soon as Sofie heard Jojo's voice, she knew that her friend was honestly upset about how she had acted.

After the phone call, Sofie thought that computers and the Internet certainly were great inventions, but that the telephone was at least as good – if not better. She was a little angry with herself for not calling Jojo earlier. If she had done that, she might not have had to be sad for so long. But on the other hand, it might have been useless talking to Jojo when she was still friends with Jessica.

That was one thing Sofie would never know, but she knew that she had done the right thing by finally calling Jojo.

Another thing that made Sofie happy was that Isabelle seemed to be alright again after the incident with Philip. It was okay to joke with her again, and the mood in the little stable was better than ever.

Sofie had actually not spoken to her cousin about the Philip incident yet, but Philip was a sensitive area and Sofie thought that it might be best to let time heal the wounds. If Isabelle wanted to talk about what had happened, she was welcome to, but Sofie was careful not to mention Philip's name when she didn't have to. She didn't want to rub salt into Isabelle's wounds. Not again.

Sofie could see that Isabelle was avoiding Josefin, which was probably for the best. Josefin, on the other hand, acted exactly the same. She seemed to be blissfully unaware of the jealous drama she had caused.

All in all, going to the stable on Monday morning really hadn't felt bad at all. Not even the fact that everybody else in the family was snuggling under their warm comforters made Sofie lose her zest for life. The joy of having Jojo back had drowned out everything else.

❉ ❉ ❉ ❉

On Tuesday, Sofie's happiness reached record height. This was because Speedy was fantastic in the qualifying race – he more or less wiped the track with his competitors!

"Speedy Legend is definitely back in business!" Tommy shouted happily when they came back. "I can tell that we're seeing the start of something big here…"

Sofie wasn't quite sure what her uncle meant by that, but she had read in Isabelle's specialist book that many trotters had their greatest successes at Speedy's age. Often by the time the horses reached five or six you could pinpoint the international stars and weed out the second-rates. Speedy didn't seem to belong in the latter category.

During dinner Sofie, almost bursting with pride, told all about Speedy's victory and what Tommy had said afterwards. Everybody in the family was happy about the gelding's success. Stefan gave Elizabeth a wink which meant, "I knew she'd take a liking to the horses," but he was tactful enough to not say it out loud.

After dinner, Sofie walked around with a big smile on her face. She had been so happy that her body felt like it was full of helium. It was impossible to sit still. Emma finally said, "Do you realize you've been grinning ever since you came home?"

"Why? Is it a problem that I'm in a good mood?" Sofie asked.

"No, but you look kind of silly. And it's somewhat irritating when somebody is this happy on a rainy Tuesday in July when it ought to be summer outside."

"I'm sorry."

Sofie kept grinning from ear to ear. Emma shook her head and went back to her crime novel.

The day after Speedy's qualifying race, Sofie sloshed into the partly muddy yard with Isabelle's old rubber boots on her feet. She lifted hopeful eyes to the sky to see if it was brightening anywhere, but all she could see were gray clouds. The clouds moved in the wind but immediately seemed to be replaced by new ones. There was no hint of sunlight anywhere.

Jenny came running from the parking lot.

"Brrrr!" she said, holding her jacket tightly closed. "I'm running away to Spain soon!"

"You are?"

"No, but I wish I could," the strawberry-blonde groom laughed.

Jenny was one of Sofie's many colleagues at Humleby Farm. She was a little heavy, and she always seemed to be in a good mood.

"My vacation is short this year so I guess making it to Stockholm is the best I can hope for," she went on.

"It's supposed to be a beautiful city." Sofie felt a little silly for never having visited Sweden's capital, but on the other hand, she had lived in England's capital for ten years, which really wasn't bad.

"It is," Jenny cheerfully assured her, "but the weather is often like this. I wish I had the time and money to go someplace where sun is guaranteed."

Jenny worked in the upper stable with Daniel and Fredrik. Just like Sofie, she cleaned out the stalls and took care of the horses, but she also had one more job: riding them. Humleby Farm was a stable for trotters and all the horses were hot-blooded trotters, bred to be driven. But one part of Tommy's philosophy was that the horses should be ridden every now and then, to give the muscle groups not used when driving a workout. These riding sessions turned out to be a good complement to the rest of the training, and Jenny had a lot to do.

They reached the end of the passage between the stable and the garage.

"Would you like to come riding soon?" Jenny asked when she was in the doorway to the upper stable.

"What?" Sofie wasn't sure if she had heard correctly.

Jenny laughed. "If you want to, you can try riding. I can teach you the basics some day when I have the time."

Sofie felt a little dizzy. It was one thing to lead a horse to or from a paddock or to groom it when it was tied up in the passageway, but riding was completely another matter! She had never tried riding in her life, and the thought of sitting on a horse's back was scary and tempting. She couldn't say a word.

Jenny stood in the doorway to get out of the persistent rain. She went on, "Riding a trotter isn't like riding a riding school horse. It's a little bouncier... but just as much fun!" She smiled. "Think about it. I promise you won't have to start with Rocky or Duke."

Duke was the other stallion in the stable.

"O-okay," Sofie stuttered, staggering into the little stable.

She could go riding! But did she really want to? Everything was happening so fast she didn't have time to think. Maybe that was just as well.

"Iiihaaahaaa!" Oh My Gosh put his head out through the opening above the stall door.

"Good morning!" Sofie reached out and scratched the brown gelding between his ears.

"Just think, I might get to ride you some day," Sofie told him. "Would you like that?"

Oh My Gosh snorted. Sofie didn't really know how to interpret this answer. She smiled and kept scratching him.

Just then Tina and Isabelle came into the passageway. They seemed to be happy about something and were talking eagerly.

"Do you think he'll be there?" Isabelle asked, her eyes sparkling. For a moment Sofie thought that they were talking about Philip, but then she realized that the conversation was about another guy; a chestnut gelding named Speedy Legend.

"He'll have to, considering how well he did yesterday." Tina smiled. "He's at the same level as just before he was injured. It's so unbelievable. I th –"

"Is Speedy going to be in a race?" Curiosity made Sofie forget her manners, and she interrupted Tina in mid-sentence. Her older colleague didn't seem to mind.

"And good morning to you!" she said, winking at Sofie.

"Good morning." Sofie blushed a little. "Uh… you were talking about Speedy, right?"

"Congratulations! You just won a medal for eaves-dropping," Isabelle quipped.

Sofie stuck her tongue out at her cousin.

"Quit it," she said. "What were you talking about? Is it secret?"

"Not at all," Tina said, walking over to the tin cupboards at the end of the passageway. She came back with a bridle over her arm. "Tommy is sending in Speedy's name for the Skåne Mastership."

Sofie gave Tina a questioning look.

"It's a really good race, with lots of top horses. Not world-class stuff, but still a good deal of money. And lots of spectators."

"Sounds great! When is it?"

Sofie hoped that this one would be an evening race – then maybe she could go. Maybe she could even go as Tina's "helper." Imagine seeing Speedy in a real race!

"In three weeks," Tina said, opening the door to Rocky's stall. "I think it's August 20th. A Tuesday evening."

Sofie shouted for joy inside. Speedy's first race in a year! This would be the greatest event of the summer.

Tina went to bridle Rocky who, as usual, made a little fuss before his keeper could sure-handedly lead him out into the passageway and tie him up.

"Isabelle and I are going to the track with Rocky and Tornado. Can you take Champ and Oh My Gosh out?"

"Will do," Sofie started immediately.

Tina got one harness for Rocky and gave another to Isabelle, who had just tied Tornado further down in the passageway.

"We'll be back for the morning meeting. After that, we'll go get Speedy and the gang," Tina told Sofie.

"Okay." Sofie went in to Oh My Gosh and attached his lead rein. She carefully pressed against the brown gelding's shoulder until he turned around in his stall. Then she led him out into the passageway.

"I'll take one at a time." She turned to Tina.

"That's fine." Tina tightened the girth under Rocky's stomach. The stallion protested by neighing and scraping his hoof on the floor. Tina patted the restless horse on his neck. "If you want to train, you'll have to put up with some preparation," she said.

Rocky snorted softly, as if he was mumbling an answer.

The morning passed quickly. Sofie's thoughts were filled with making up with Jojo – but she was also thinking

114

about the race that Speedy was going to run. It would be so exciting to see him in action on the track. Sofie was sure that Speedy would beat his competitors, at least when it came to beauty – and by several horse-lengths!

When Sofie came back to the stable after her lunch break, fortified by Elizabeth's homemade meatballs, she started right in on her afternoon chores. The stalls of the indoor horses needed to be mucked out, and it was time to polish all the harnesses and bridles.

Isabelle showed up a few minutes later and they worked quickly and efficiently, discussing everything from Sofie's possible riding lessons to the latest Kelly Clarkson song to Speedy's big comeback in August.

While Sofie carefully greased a harness, she thought that she could hardly have a better time than this. She had a summer job that she loved, nice friends at work, a friend in the same village and a best friend in London. There was nothing to complain about!

But when Sofie tied Speedy up in the passageway, just before they were to take the outside horses back to their stalls, she suddenly had a feeling that something was wrong. Speedy wasn't acting like his usual self.

"Look at him!" she exclaimed, gesturing for Isabelle to come over. "Doesn't he look kind of — I don't know – queasy?"

Isabelle watched the chestnut trotter for a moment and then said, "You think? I think he looks normal."

She went up to the horse and patted the bridge of his nose. "Are you queasy?" she asked, kissing the gelding's muzzle.

Speedy lifted his head and silently watched Isabelle.

"There's something about his eyes…" Sofie couldn't really pinpoint what was wrong, but it was almost as if he wasn't quite there.

"Pooh!" Isabelle said, returning to Star. "You're just imagining things."

"Maybe …" Sofie kept grooming Speedy's reddish brown mane. The chestnut stood very still while she worked through every inch of his coat.

"He sure is enjoying your spa treatment!" Isabelle called from her spot a bit further up the passageway. "There's nothing wrong with him. He seems happy enough."

Yet no matter how much Sofie tried, she couldn't let go of the thought that something was wrong. She decided to ask Tina to have a look at Speedy before they let him out in the paddock.

Time to choose

Tina finally persuaded Sofie that there was nothing at all wrong with Speedy. He had eaten and, according to her, seemed to be as healthy as, well, a horse.

Sofie knew that she had to take Tina's word for it. It was Tina who had fifteen years of experience working with horses, not Sofie.

Walking home from the stable that afternoon, Sofie managed to shake off her worry and thought about something a lot more interesting instead – her upcoming trip to London! She had made the decision that week, maybe even right after the phone call. Sofie now felt sure that she wanted to see Jojo, yet she still hadn't said anything to her parents. Last Friday she had said that she would *not* go to London, and Sofie knew that her dad would question her change of heart.

"How can I be sure you won't change your mind again?" he would ask, making an exasperated face.

The same day as the phone call, Sofie had sent a new e-mail to Jojo. She wrote that her parents were counting on Sofie visiting, and suggested a week in August. Then Sofie had told Emma that she was probably going to London anyway, and her big sister said something about taking it easy. But Sofie didn't want to listen to that. Why should she take it easy? She knew Jojo better than anybody else.

Sofie decided to bring up her trip that night during dinner. It was more than a week since they'd discussed it, and she knew that Emma would be away all evening. That meant that her sister couldn't meddle in Sofie's plans.

"But you just said you weren't going!" Stefan looked at his youngest daughter in confusion.

"Yes, I know," Sofie said calmly, reaching for the butter. "But I've changed my mind."

"But are you absolutely sure you want to go, now?"

"Yes, I'm sure." Sofie grabbed a piece of bread and started buttering it.

"And how can I be sure you won't change your mind again tomorrow?" Stefan leaned back and looked at Sofie, his forehead wrinkled .

"I won't," Sofie said firmly.

"You can't cancel those cheap tickets that you buy on the Internet, you know," Stefan pointed out. He looked at his wife, hoping for some kind of support, and he got it.

"Sofie…" Elizabeth smiled her best let's-not-quarrel-but-talk-calmly-and-sensibly-smile. "I understand that you're glad that you and Joanna are friends again, but isn't it a little rushed to book the trip right now? Wouldn't it be better to wait for a week or two, to see how things work out? Or maybe wait until the next vacation?"

Sofie put her milk glass down on the table with a bang. Parents could be so hopeless sometimes!

"*You're* not the ones who spoke to Jojo! She's said she's sorry! She's very sorry for being such a jerk."

"I don't doubt that." Elizabeth put one hand on Sofie's shoulder and went on, "But I still think it would be best if you were in contact for a while longer before we buy a ticket. So we can be sure it won't happen again. And also, I want to call Joanna's parents and ask them what they think."

Sofie shook off her mom's hand.

"They've already said that it's all right for me to come! And if we don't book a ticket now, there won't be any left! And I won't get to London although I'm working in the stable from morning till night every day! Or maybe that's what you want?" She glared at her parents.

"One single ticket can always be found," her dad said. "If push came to shove, I'm sure you could buy one the day before your trip. Don't rush into anything now. Suppose you buy a ticket today and fall out with Joanna again tomorrow… it would be like throwing your money away!"

Sofie could feel anger growing within her. Now, when she'd finally decided to go, it felt like this trip was a matter of life or death. At least life or death for her and Jojo's friendship.

"I get to decide what I do with my own money!" Sofie hissed.

"No, Sofie, actually you don't." Stefan was starting to sound irritated. "You're not of age yet."

Sofie violently rose from her chair and pushed it against the table, forcefully enough that cups and glasses almost fell over.

"You don't understand anything!" She ran out of the kitchen, up the stairs and into her room, banging the door shut behind her.

Why were parents this awful? First, they made her

119

work in a stable so she could make her own money for an airplane ticket. And then they refused to let her book her ticket! Sofie threw herself on the bed and cried in her pillow. Life was so endlessly unfair!

After about twenty minutes, there was a faint knock on the door. She pretended not to hear. It was probably Elizabeth, wanting to explain her view and try to make Sofie understand.

Sofie didn't want to understand. And she couldn't see that there was anything to explain.

A minute later, there was a new knock and the door opened a crack. Sofie lay still on the bed and pretended to be asleep. The door slowly closed.

She breathed out. The last thing she wanted right now was to listen to one of Elizabeth's endless now-we-have-to-talk-this-through sermons. Instead, she got up from the bed and turned the computer on. She was going to print the e-mail where Jojo had mentioned that her parents had said that it was OK for Sofie to come there. Then she'd sneak downstairs and put the printout on the kitchen table. That would show them that there were no obstacles to her going to London!

Before she printed the message, she quickly read it through and everything seemed to be clear. But when she came to the last line, she suddenly sat up straight:

Mom says it would be best if you came here the week before school begins. We are going to Brighton with friends the week before that…

Oh, no! Sofie read the e-mail one more time and realized that there was a *big* conflict. Speedy was running his race on the twentieth, the week before school started! That was the day of his big comeback! She hit one hand on her desk hard enough to hurt.

What would she do now? Sofie rubbed her aching hand and thought wildly.

Considering her parents' view of things, it would have been easy to skip the trip and blame everything on them. Then she wouldn't miss Speedy's race.

But she suspected that that might mean a certain risk that she would lose Jojo's friendship instead, and after all this was more important to her than Speedy's race. There would be more races with Speedy in them. Sofie was sure about that.

Her brain worked at full speed. One second she was totally sure that she would keep trying to persuade her parents to let her book her trip right away, but the next second she was sure Speedy would fail horribly if she wasn't there with him when his big moment came!

She couldn't sort out her conflicting feelings. As soon as she thought she really knew what she wanted, a new thought fluttered by and made her change her mind. Some of the thoughts were about Jessica. What if Jojo and Jessica became friends again? And what if Jojo thought that all three of them ought to be together when Sofie came to visit?

For a while, she almost thought that her parents were right about the trip to London. Maybe it would be better to wait? Could she really trust Jojo? But then she was ashamed for even thinking something like that. Wasn't it just a bad excuse, making it possible to stay at home with Speedy? Or maybe because she was worrying about Jessica?

Finally, Sofie decided to go out for some fresh air. Maybe her head would clear if she went for a short walk. She found a light sweater, draped it over her shoulders and knotted the sleeves over her front. Then she silently went down the stairs, put her feet in her sneakers and slid out through the door.

Sofie went out on the road, walked around their yard and kept on walking, without thinking, toward the paddocks furthest away. It was as if as some invisible force was pulling her closer to Speedy.

The evening was wonderful. It had stopped drizzling and felt warmer outside. Sofie turned onto the gravel road between the paddocks and listened to the calming evening sounds. Crickets were playing in the grass, a pheasant called somewhere and every now and then you could hear the muted sound of hooves pattering on the ground. The horses always acted up a little when somebody came walking down the road.

Before her, the horizon looked like a great mouth, swallowing an enormous piece of glowing sun candy. Silhouetted against the sunset, she could see Speedy and Sky where they grazed. She walked faster down the hill.

"Hi, boys!"

The two horses stopped to listen. Sky turned his head in the direction of the sound and neighed softly when he saw her.

When Sofie reached to the fence, she was met by the dark brown gelding who had trotted up to meet her. She smiled and let him smell her fingers.

"What's up?" she asked.

The horse answered by neighing softly again.

"You seem do be doing fine," Sofie noted. She patted Sky's neck and stroked his black mane.

Soon, Speedy was also by the fence. His coat shone in the last golden sunrays of the evening and Sofie couldn't

help but think that he actually looked like a fairytale horse. He really *was* as unbelievably beautiful as in the newspaper photos.

"Hi there, Speedy Legend!" Sofie reached out and patted the bridge of his nose. "I wish you could tell me what to do," she sighed.

Speedy neighed softly and looked at her with his dark, inscrutable eyes.

"I guess I should decide to go to Jojo's…" Sofie went on, resting one cheek against the gelding's neck. "But she isn't the one who supported me this summer, you are. And that's why I want to be with you when you need support."

Deep within herself, Sofie knew that Speedy would manage just fine without her on the day of the race, but the thought that he just might need her felt good.

Suspicions confirmed

The major result of Sofie's evening walk was the big scolding she got later.

"You have to tell us when you go out!" was the blunt and to the point message that Elizabeth angrily delivered when Sofie came in through the door.

After that, she had been given an endless explanation as to why her parents wanted her to wait to book her ticket to London.

She simply nodded before she went upstairs to bed. Somewhere deep inside, Sofie knew that there was a certain logic to her parents' point of view. Over and over, they'd repeated that she ought to wait to order the ticket, for her own sake. That way she wouldn't have to be disappointed again, and totally broke.

Furthermore, Stefan promised to "personally deliver her to England by car" if every ticket to London was sold in two weeks' time, which meant the problem was actually solved. She could go.

It was just that Speedy's race kept nagging at the back of her brain. Sofie and Speedy belonged together. This feeling had overwhelmed her ever since Speedy came to Humleby Farm.

Sofie was sitting on the bed of the light blue pickup truck, heading for Speedy's paddock. Fredrik, Josefin and Ewa, one of the middle stable grooms, were talking but Sofie was absorbed in her own thoughts. She was nervous. Tina had given her a new task – bringing both Speedy and Sky back, by herself.

Sofie was both proud and scared.

"B-but… do you really think I can manage?" She felt cold sweat oozing into her palms.

"I wouldn't ask you if I didn't." Tina smiled. "And you know that both Speedy and Sky are as calm and sweet as can be."

Sofie nodded. "Well, yes…"

"Good, then it's settled!"

And it had been.

It was an unusually fine morning. The summer warmth seemed to have decided to return – with a vengeance. Sofie could feel the sun burning against her dark blue T-shirt, and it wasn't even seven o'clock yet. She leaned back as far as she could, closed her eyes, and didn't open them until Roger braked hard at the far paddock.

Everybody jumped off the truck, taking aim for "their" horses, and that was the moment – right when Sofie landed on the grass on her feet with a soft thud – that she saw him.

"Help!" she screamed. "Help!"

In a matter of seconds, Sofie had managed to wrench the gate open and run into the paddock. What she saw made her entire body tremble: her beloved Speedy was lying down close to the lean-to, but it didn't look as if he was resting.

The chestnut gelding seemed lifeless. He was lying on his side with his neck stretched out from his body – and he was very still.

Sofie dropped down to his side.

"Oh, no!" she yelled. "I knew it! I knew something was wrong!"

The other grooms had heard Sofie's despairing scream and weren't far behind. Fredrik was the one who got to her first.

"He's dead!" Sofie sobbed, feeling the horror welling up within her. "Speedy's dead!"

Fredrik quickly bent over and placed his thumb and forefinger on the fetlock of Speedy's left foreleg.

"No," he said tightly, "Speedy isn't dead, but his pulse is uneven and he's hot. We have to get a vet here quickly!"

To her great relief, Sofie realized he was right when Speedy suddenly lifted one eyelid and immediately let it fall shut again.

Fredrik quickly grabbed the phone in his jeans pocket and dialed Tommy's number. It wasn't long before somebody answered. Fredrik quickly explained the situation and hung up.

"Tommy's calling Andersson right away!"

Andersson was the veterinarian that Humleby Farm used.

Roger, who had heard the commotion and jumped out of the car, was ordered to drive back to the farm to get Tommy or Maggie.

"Do you want to come along, Sofie?" He gestured to the pickup. "You look a little pale."

"Sky can stay here with Speedy," Ewa interjected. "So you don't have to worry about him."

127

Sofie, who was still kneeling next to Speedy, met Roger's eyes.

"Thanks, but I want to stay here."

Roger nodded and went back to the car.

Ewa, Fredrik and Josefin stayed, watching the beautiful animal that was lying in the grass right by their feet. The horse's eyes were closed and he seemed only vaguely aware of them.

Sky moved uneasily around them, neighing incessantly.

"What can be the matter with him?" Ewa bent down and cautiously felt Speedy's legs, one at a time. She looked at his hooves and carefully felt his belly.

"No idea," Fredrik said. "Yesterday, he seemed fit and spry."

Sofie wanted to protest, to scream that if somebody had listened to her yesterday this would never had happened! Still, she knew that there had been no obvious signs of illness yesterday afternoon. Speedy hadn't been hot then, and he had eaten and drunk plenty of water. She had just had that feeling that something was wrong.

"I wonder how long he's been lying like this," Josefin seemed worried.

Sofie knew that horses shouldn't lie too long in the same position, since their inner organs are squeezed.

"He was okay at about eleven last night," she mumbled, trying to hold back her tears. "I was here then."

While the others discussed Speedy's current state, talking about whether they should turn him over or try to get him to stand up, Sofie stroked his hot neck and chanted endlessly.

"Don't give up, Speedy. You have to get through this! I'll do anything just to get you healthy again."

Suddenly, the chestnut twitched and started throwing himself back and forth on the ground. Sofie moved back and fell over, but Fredrik moved in quickly and got her to her feet.

"Look out!" He pushed Sofie away from Speedy just as a hoof came lashing out in her direction, missing her by inches.

The chestnut gelding neighed shrilly and rolled back and forth as if he had been stung by an entire swarm of bees. It looked horrible.

"Oh my gosh!" Josefin put her hands to her face in terror and squinted at Speedy through her fingers.

"So where's Andersson?" Fredrik looked around in worry.

Ewa was as white as a sheet. Sofie stood next to them and watched in despair as her favorite horse squirmed in pain. What was the matter with him?

From the time that Sofie discovered Speedy on the ground to the time Andersson arrived and did his examination seemed like an eternity.

Tommy and Andersson both arrived about twenty minutes after Fredrik had called. Just a few moments before the vet arrived Speedy, as if by magic, had calmed and lain on his side again. Everybody started talking at the same time trying to tell Andersson about Speedy's sudden fit. The vet listened carefully while he hurried toward his patient.

Fredrik went over and stood next to Sofie. He put one hand on her shoulder.

"It's going to be all right," he whispered, but Sofie didn't think that he sounded really sure.

Everybody in the paddock was very tense while the vet worked. Nobody said anything, and the only thing that broke the weird silence was Sky's uneasy neighing. The dark brown gelding seemed as worried about his friend as the human beings around him.

Andersson worked quickly and efficiently. First he took Speedy's pulse, then his temperature. After that he felt Speedy's belly. The last thing he did was to carefully pry open the chestnut's jaws and examine his teeth and gums.

Sofie shuddered when she saw Andersson take a tangle of see-through plastic tubes out of his bag. Would Speedy be given an intravenous drip right here in the paddock? Sofie almost got dizzy, looking at the long needle, but Speedy didn't seem to care what Andersson did. The horse lay very still, with eyes closed, as if he was sound asleep.

When the vet finally delivered his verdict Sofie held her breath. Fredrik, who hadn't let go of Sofie's shoulder, hugged it tightly.

"You can all relax." Andersson wiped his forehead with a handkerchief and turned to Tommy. "Speedy has colic," he went on. "He lashed out due to the stomach pain. And considering how he acted right before I arrived, I'd say it's gas colic. It looks terrible, but he'll be better very soon. I've given him some medicine to ease the cramps, and just to be on the safe side I've given him a drip in case he's constipated."

"What caused the colic?" Tommy asked. "Do you have any idea?"

Andersson wiped his brow again.

"Hard to say," he said. "There are many causes of colic. Did you change his fodder?"

Tommy shook his head.

"No, I've given him the same kind of fodder since he came here."

The vet shrugged.

"He may have eaten something unsuitable. Maybe a poisonous plant?"

"But…" Tommy looked around in the paddock. "There's only grass and clover here… How could Speedy have eaten anything poisonous? And anyway, I thought horses usually avoid poisonous plants."

Andersson nodded.

"Mostly they do," he agreed. "But somebody may have passed by and fed the horse. Given him a handful of grass and maybe something else by accident." The vet nodded at the woods behind the paddocks. "This somebody probably had no idea that horses can't eat everything that grows outside."

Sofie suddenly thought of the small boys that she and Isabelle had seen sneaking around the woods. She also remembered what Isabelle had said at the time. Something about her hoping that the boys wouldn't hurt the horses in any way…

"Uh…" Sofie cleared her throat. Maybe this wasn't important at all, but she still collected herself and went on. "Isabelle and I saw a couple of young boys hiding in the woods a while back… Maybe they were the ones who fed Speedy?"

Tommy turned to her, looking interested.

"It might well be. Have you seen them again? Do you know who they are?"

Sofie shook her head.

"No idea, unfortunately… They weren't very old, about eight or nine, I'd guess."

"Did anybody else see anything?" Tommy's eyes went from one groom to the next. Fredrik shook his head, as did Ewa. Josefin looked thoughtful.

132

"Well, when I think about it, I guess I've seen a couple of kids running around the woods," she said after a while. "But I don't think I've seen them this week…"

"Well, as long as it doesn't happen again…" Tommy looked out across the paddock. "We'll have to hope that this was a one-time thing. I can't just hire a security company to watch the horses twenty-four seven." He turned to the vet. "What do we do now?"

"Speedy has a slight temperature. In this unbearable heat, that makes him seem worse than he really is," Andersson explained. "But he has a drip and I expect him to come around quite soon. Take him inside today and let him rest. You might want to deworm him, too. Just as a precaution. As I said, I'm not exactly sure what caused his colic. It might be something he ate, but it might be something else."

"Should we feed him as usual?" Tommy asked.

"As soon as he *wants* to eat… I don't think he's very hungry right now," the vet said as he started to pack up his things.

Sofie had never thought that she would be this happy about anybody being constipated. She almost ran right up to Dr. Andersson to kiss him on his mouth. Luckily, she checked herself and walked up to Speedy instead. She bent over and carefully kissed his neck.

"I knew I could trust you," she whispered into his straw-colored mane.

Roger and Tommy had planned ahead and brought a trailer to the paddock. When the drip started having its effect, Speedy rose by himself and Tommy was able to lead him into the transport.

Andersson looked satisfied. He had been walking to

his car, but stopped and watched as the trotter was put in the trailer.

"The fact that Speedy stood up so quickly is a good sign," he said. "He's going to be all right."

Everybody went back to work. Ewa offered to take Sky to the stable, and Sofie said yes, so as not to seem disagreeable. She was a little weak in her knees after the experience but she was still sure that she would have managed to lead a calm horse like Sky.

"It's a good thing it wasn't worse!" Fredrik turned and smiled at Sofie. She was walking back to the stable with the apprentice and two of the horses from the upper stable.

Sofie nodded seriously. "Yes, it was horrible. At first, I actually thought he was dead… And then I thought he *would* die!" She suddenly thought of something. "What about the race?" she said.

"I think he'll be fine. When is it?"

"August twentieth," Sofie said, immediately remembering her big problem.

Fredrik counted on his fingers.

"Well, if it's what Dr. Andersson thinks, that Speedy just ate something bad for him, he'll be better by tomorrow. He probably ought to take it easy for a couple of days, but I don't think it will impact the race… It's almost three weeks away! As long as he doesn't need antibiotics, everything's cool."

Sofie gave Fredrik a questioning look.

The apprentice went on, "A horse can't be given antibiotics just before a race. It has to be free of medical treatment for at least two weeks in order to be allowed to start," he explained. "Well, the number of days differs a little, depending on what kind of medicine has been used."

134

Sofie nodded thoughtfully. For her sake, it would have been just as well if Speedy had missed that race. Then she wouldn't have had to think about what to do about her trip to London. Still, of course she wanted Speedy to get well as quickly as possible.

Then there was the fact that Tommy and Tina had said that the Skåne Mastership was a perfect first race for Speedy after his long hiatus, and Sofie wanted nothing more than for her beautiful favorite to do well.

Sofie and Fredrik had just walked into the yard when there was a beep in Sofie's pocket. She quickly took out her cell phone and saw that she had received a text message. The number was very familiar.

Call me as soon as you can! /Jojo

The big day

"Hurry up! I promise, the horses are going to think you're beautiful!" Sofie looked impatiently at the kitchen clock, which indicated that it was almost quarter to four.

Jojo stuck her tongue out at Sofie and calmly kept combing her hair in front of the big mirror in the hall.

"Well, I'm done now," she said, putting her feet in her sneakers. "Let's go."

As soon as they went outside onto the front steps, the hot afternoon sun beat down on them.

"Phew! I'm sweaty already," Jojo complained.

Sofie walked to the corner of the house and waved to Elizabeth, who was kneeling in front of one of the dazzling flowerbeds. "Goodbye, Mom!" she called. "We're off now."

Elizabeth looked up and waved at the girls.

"Bye! See you there!"

This was the day with a capital D; the day when Speedy would make his comeback and finally get to prove that he was still one of the elite Swedish trotters. Nobody in the village wanted to miss out on the big event. Rumors had spread like wildfire – and the papers had helped by publishing two more articles about "The Fantastic Speedy Legend." Tommy and Speedy had even been on TV a couple of times.

Elizabeth and Stefan were coming down to Jägersro later that evening, and bringing the neighbors. Of course, the entire Sandberg family would be seated in a box right on the track, as well as several of the grooms at Humleby Farm.

Emma had gone back to London the day before. She actually seemed disappointed that she couldn't be there to root for Speedy, but she had to start preparing for a new term at the university and her plane ticket had been booked for a long time.

Soon, the girls were walking along the village road. Sofie stole a glance at Jojo. It felt so unbelievably great to have her friend walking next to her. Sofie had never seen Jojo surrounded by birch trees and green pastures. It was almost as out of place as a cow in the middle of London!

Everything had happened so fast. When Sofie called Jojo on that hot July day, the same day that Speedy had come down with colic, she had been incredibly nervous. Why had the message told her to hurry? Had Jojo changed her mind about the trip?

It turned out that Jojo's grandma, who lived in Sweden, had fallen and broken her leg. Because of this, Jojo's parents had decided to go home and help her for a couple of weeks. Jojo's grandma lived outside of Stockholm, and when the Nilssons went back to England, Jojo caught a flight to visit Sofie.

Jojo had been in Humleby for three days now, and Sofie marveled at how quickly they had bonded. Sofie, who had finished her summer job at Humleby Farm, brought her best friend to the stable on her very first day in town. She proudly showed off her new knowledge, and Jojo was actually impressed.

"This is crazy, Sofie," Jojo laughed. "You used to be so scared of horses!"

"I know!" Sofie laughed with her. "And now, here I am, helping out *voluntarily!* Almost every day!"

On the second night, when they were talking in bed, Sofie mustered her courage and asked Jojo what she thought about her newfound interest.

Jojo had lain quietly in the dark for quite a while; long enough to make Sofie nervous about the answer.

"You know, Sofie…" Jojo had finally said. "I think you're brave *and* cool."

Sofie breathed out a sigh of relief and let Jojo continue.

"I'm not sure that I would have fought to overcome my fear as hard as you did. I mean, I'm scared of horses… I think I would have refused to go there."

"It was the only job I could get," Sofie had pointed out, looking at the black sky. She had forgotten to close the blinds, so she could see the stars glittering outside.

"Yes, I know…" Jojo had fallen silent. "But still. I would have been terribly nervous."

"I *was* terribly nervous," Sofie assured her. "But it was the only way to make it to London. Mom and Dad didn't want to pay for a trip before the holidays."

"I admire you," Jojo said. "Not just because you overcame your fear, but because you actually can stand those smelly creatures."

Then they giggled and Sofie threw a pillow in her friend's face.

The girls hurried into the stable yard. There still were
several cars in the parking lot, but in just fifteen minutes
most of them would be gone. The day was ending for most
of the workers at Humleby Farm.

In the middle of the yard was a horse trailer with its
driver's side door open. Sofie turned to see Tina come
running from the stable.

"Hi girls!" the groom said when she got closer. "You can
ride with me if you want. Isabelle is going with Tommy and
Maggie."

"Great!" Sofie could feel a tingling in her stomach.
"How is he?" she asked.

"Tommy's just fine, as far as I know." Tina grinned and
jumped into the driver's seat.

"I mean Speedy, and you know it!" Sofie laughed. She
and Jojo squeezed in next to Tina and closed the door.

Tina smiled.

"Speedy seems to be in great shape," she said, slowly
turning out onto the village road. "I just hope I brought
everything," she went on, glancing in the rear view mirror.
"I was in somewhat of a hurry."

Sofie looked out through the window. Soon, they passed
the paddocks on the left side and she caught a glimpse of
Sky, standing in the shadow of the lean-to. Due to the great
late summer weather, Tina thought that there would be a
big audience in the stands. She also thought that the media
attention Speedy had picked up in the last weeks would
attract a lot of people.

Sofie couldn't believe that the day finally had come!
Speedy would be in a race! He had never been in any great
danger – Andersson had been right. Just a day after the

139

dramatic event in the paddock, Speedy was back to his old self again. As a precaution, he had been put in the walker to give him an easy training for a couple of days before they took him to train on the big course.

At first, Tommy had been a little worried that the colic would exhaust Speedy, but as soon as training started again Speedy had run fast and his pulse had been even and steady. For the last week, he had been in the same great shape as he had before his colic.

A few days after Speedy's colic, Sofie and Isabelle had run into the two young boys close to the woods. Isabelle had asked them if they had fed the horses, and then told them, very dramatically, what had happened to Speedy.

Maybe the boys had had something to do with the incident, but Sofie was sure that they wouldn't be giving the horses anything but grass after that. And anyway, it didn't seem as if they had meant to harm anybody, that is, if they'd even been involved.

The boys lived in the high-rise apartments in the village and had just been looking for adventure at Humleby Farm. Sofie could tell that they found it exciting to sneak around in the woods – the boys probably imagined that it was a big forest, surrounded by dangerous predators.

Tina turned into the stable area behind the track. There was a lot of activity: horse transports where parked all over, and everywhere you looked you could see newly groomed horses and sulkies with drivers in colorful uniforms. Many of the grooms and trainers were warming up their protégés.

To the left of the stable area was a tall building that contained the track offices and a couple of different restaurants. They caught a glimpse of the oval track in front of the building. Above the din of voices and neighing they could hear an announcer pattering off information about the different races over the PA system.

"Wow!" Sofie exclaimed. "It's so big!"

Tina nodded and braked in front of Humleby Farm's racing stable. All the professional trainers who used Jägersro as their home track rented a stable by the course. That way they could groom, feed and check the horses before and after the races, and there was also room for the drivers and grooms to change clothes and relax.

Jojo and Sofie jumped out of the car. Tina opened the rear doors and gave the girls one big bag each.

"Can you carry these inside, please?" She took two more big bags herself. They put everything close to the stall where Speedy would be waiting for his race. Tina went back to the transport and led the evening's main attraction out. Sofie drew a breath.

"Oh!" she said, watching her chestnut favorite with big round eyes. His coat shone like velvet and his blond mane was braided with a rubber band, the same red color as Humleby Farm's competition uniforms.

Ewa, Fredrik and another apprentice at the stable, Mattias, came out of the stable. They were there to take care of Duke, who was starting in the apprentices' race just before Speedy's race.

"Hi there! I see the big celebrity has finally made his entrance! I'm afraid I didn't have time to lay out the red carpet," Fredrik joked.

"That's too bad," Tina said, pretending to be serious. "It'll mean a deduction in your pay."

Fredrik grinned.

When Philip appeared from out of nowhere, Sofie got tense, but then she remembered that he was actually driving

Speedy, since it was a special occasion. Too bad she'd just managed to forget everything that had happened a few weeks back.

"What a hunk," Jojo whispered in Sofie's ear.

"Oh, no!" Sofie moaned, making a nasty face. "Not you, too!"

"What? What do you mean by that?" Jojo asked curiously.

"I'll tell you some other time." Sofie pushed her friend into the stable passageway.

Tina had wrapped Speedy's legs carefully to avoid injuries in the transport. She asked Sofie to remove the wraps while she put his bridle and harness on.

Jojo stood in the stall door and leaned against the doorframe, watching what Tina and Sofie were doing inside the stall curiously.

"When is his race?" she asked.

"He'll be starting at seven," Tina said with her body in a strange angle, half hidden under Speedy. She was adjusting something on the harness that seemed to have gotten off-kilter.

Jojo looked surprised.

"At seven? Why are we here this early?"

Tina smiled. "You just wait, we have a lot to do before the race! First I'll warm him up outside, then it's time for the driver to try him out on the course, and in between that we have to take good care of him." She stood up and patted the elegant chestnut. "Can you tell how calm he is?" she went on. "Ready but calm. Things are going to be fine!"

She led Speedy out into the passageway and asked Ewa to get a long sulky.

While Tina was warming Speedy up, Sofie and Jojo

142

went out in the yard and looked around. They sneaked in next to the track to see if the audience was there yet.

"Wow! Look!" Sofie let her eyes follow the long side of the stands in front of the tall building. The first race hadn't even started yet and there were people everywhere – behind the glass wall and in front of it. She had never imagined that there would be this many people.

"Great!" Jojo said.

"Yeah…" Sofie hesitated a little. "But if he makes a poor showing, there are *so many* people who will see it." She was starting to feel nervous for Speedy.

"He won't make a poor showing," Jojo said with absolute certainty, putting her arm around Sofie's shoulders.

Sofie smiled. Jojo was one of the most reassuring people she knew. Especially in these kinds of situations.

When it was almost time for Speedy's race, the entire Sandberg family, Sofie's parents and many of the grooms from Humleby Farm finally showed up. A couple of reporters had stopped by and Speedy's owner Axel was also there. George and his wife stood outside the stable with the others. Sofie was surprised when she saw that even old Tom had made it down to the track.

Despite the warning from Tina, she was still surprised about the amount of preparation before the race. Tina worked without a break – quickly and efficiently. You could tell that she had done all this many times before. Sofie helped out as best she could, but a lot of stuff was new to her so she tried to watch and learn.

Speedy would be wearing blinders that Philip could adjust if he needed to by pulling on a string, so that Speedy wouldn't look to the sides and get spooked. Tina also put pull wads in Speedy's ears. Philip could yank these out by pulling on a couple of other strings, which was supposed to give Speedy a boost of extra power at the final turn. It was important that the correct set of strings was hanging on the correct side of the horse.

"The driver shouldn't have to worry about which strings are which," Tina explained.

"But what are you *doing*!?" Jojo exclaimed when Tina, after the last warm-up, wrapped most of Speedy's legs with see-through plastic. "He can't look like that, can he?"

Tina laughed out loud.

"There's ointment underneath and plastic film on top of that. It's all to make his joints as soft and warm as possible."

Jojo shook her head.

"I promise to remove the plastic before the race," Tina said, grinning broadly.

They took a short break to watch Duke's race on a little TV set that was mounted to the wall in the passageway. The stallion had a good start, but lost some headway during the finish and came in third. Everybody thought it was a good result, but Sofie knew that Fredrik, who was driving, was disappointed. To Fredrik, only winning counted; he was a very competitive person.

Sofie listened with one ear to a conversation being had by the group of people outside the stable.

"What chance does Speedy have?" Stefan asked. "What's his competition like?"

"It might be tough, and also he's at track seven which isn't really great," Tommy explained. "But I think Speedy has a good chance of winning anyway. Philip will be driving him, and that's good," he went on.

Isabelle turned slightly pink when Philip was mentioned, but she seemed to be trying to shake her feelings off as well as she could.

Speedy was so beautiful, but as luck would have it, he lay down in the shavings just before they took the plastic off his legs. Suddenly he looked more like a stray dog than an elegant trotter. Tina very quickly brushed her protégé, begging him not to lie down again before the race.

Once she was finished she moved the chestnut gelding so he was standing outside the stable, newly groomed and with mane and tail combed. He wore a newly greased harness with a blue number saddle pad, his braid was in place and he calmly looked at them with his dark eyes, as if unmoved by all the excitement.

When Tina gave the reins to Philip it felt like a solemn occasion. Sofie was proud to know the most beautiful horse in the world. Philip wasn't as beautiful as Speedy but at least he looked elegant in the red uniform with *Humleby Farm* printed in yellow letters on the back.

Sofie's heart pounded with nervousness and anticipation when she saw the horse and sulky with number seven go onto the track.

"Come on!" Isabelle pushed Sofie and Jojo in front of her. "Let's go see the race!"

The rest of the group from Humleby Farm had already hurried to the track to find good places on and in front of the stands, but the girls saw Tina and a couple of the other grooms on the track area and went to stand with them instead.

The starter car drove up and the horses placed themselves behind it in two rows. The speaker kept babbling, but Sofie couldn't concentrate on what he was saying. Her eyes were nailed to Speedy and she kept her fingers crossed until her knuckles went white. How would it end? She silently prayed that he would at least not gallop. And, just for good measure, she added that it would be a good thing if he didn't finish last.

At last, they were off! Sofie was glad that Speedy was the only chestnut in the race – in spite of their numbers, she could hardly tell the other horses apart, since they were all brown.

The well-muscled animals ran along the track, at first in a group. Speedy had a fine start and advanced to fourth place during the first lap, but right after that it seemed as if he was totally blocked in by two of his brown competitors.

"Oh, no!" Sofie shouted in despair. "He can't get out!"

Tina looked tense where she was standing. Isabelle chewed her nails.

But then, at the end of the second lap, something happened: Philip found an opening and quickly made it out to the right side. In just a few seconds, number seven had advanced past two more competitors.

Sofie and Jojo were jumping up and down with excitement.

"Hurry up, Speedy!" Sofie shouted at the top of her lungs. "You can make it!"

And suddenly – without anybody really knowing how it happened – Speedy was nose to nose with the leading horse. There were just a couple of hundred yards left to the finish, and the speaker was so excited that his voice was cracking.

The audience was at least as excited as he was. The tension was unbearable! Would Speedy really win and fulfill everybody's dreams?

146

Sofie hoped that her prayers would somehow fly straight into Speedy's brain, and that they could give him one last kick.

Then one second later Jojo screamed in her ear. "Yeeesss!" she shouted. "Yes! He did it! He won!" She seemed beside herself with happiness. An unknowing observer might have thought that it was Jojo who had worked in the stable all summer and not the dark-haired girl next to her – the one looking like a living question mark.

Isabelle threw herself around Tina's neck.

"Congratulations!"

Tina's brown eyes sparkled with joy. With a big smile, she answered, "Thanks! Speedy did just what I'd hoped. And Philip too."

Isabelle smiled, somewhat stiffly. "Well, whatever you might think of him, he sure knows how to drive."

Everybody came up to congratulate Tina on the victory.

Sofie was dumbstruck, just gaping with surprise. The race had been so even that she'd barely had been able to tell which horse crossed the finish line first. She didn't have to worry for long.

"The winner is Speeeeeedy Legennnnnnd!" the speaker roared. "Hardly a nose length ahead of Dressed for Success, in second place!"

When the fact that Speedy had actually won the race slowly but surely took hold in Sofie's brain, her entire body started bubbling with joy. She threw herself around both Isabelle's and Jojo's necks, and together they danced a wild celebration dance on the grass.

After a while, Sofie let go of her friends and walked up to Tina.

"It's because of you!" Sofie was radiant with joy when

147

she smiled at her colleague. "You are the best groom in the world!" She hugged Tina.

Tina laughed.

"And I have the best helpers in the world. Don't forget that!"

Philip was given a bunch of flowers and then interviewed in front of the stands. Sofie waited impatiently as the victor marched past. All she wanted to do was see Speedy and tell him how great he was. She felt in her pocket. Yes, the apple was still there, and it would be his as soon as he was in his stall.

There were lots of people in the stable after the race. Journalists mingled with grooms, friends of the Sandberg family and people from Humleby. Philip walked around basking in the glow of success, and Sofie thought that he certainly was entitled to it this evening. For Isabelle's sake, she hoped Josefin wouldn't start kissing Philip out in the yard.

Axel, Speedy's owner, was beaming with happiness and explained that everybody who wanted to was welcome to come up to the restaurant for a glass of champagne and a snack.

"This calls for a celebration!"

Tina told Sofie to take Speedy to the shower. As she removed his sweat sheet, she wondered if Axel would have thrown all the food away if Speedy had missed the race or come in last.

Jojo sneaked into the stall.

"Do you think Axel mustered this whole celebration up just *now*," she whispered, "or was he that sure Speedy would win?"

Sofie looked at her best friend and smiled.

"Two minds, one thought," she said.

Jojo laughed until the dimple on her left cheek showed and said, "I'm glad I'm here."

"So am I," Sofie said.

Jojo got serious.

"Are you sure you've forgiven me? For all that about Jessica and me not keeping in touch?"

"Absolutely."

Jojo smiled again.

"We'll always be friends!" she declared.

Sofie knew that there was no guarantee that their friendship would last forever, but she enjoyed being with Jojo on a day like this.

"Always," she said, meeting Jojo's eyes. Then she looked at Speedy, feeling an incredible joy that she hadn't had to choose between him and her best friend.

Speedy neighed, as if he had read her thoughts and agreed that life couldn't get much better than this.

Thanks!

Thanks to...

... Hans and Mai Adielsson for letting me sneak around in their stables.

... all the grooms in those stables who patiently answered my questions.

... veterinarian Björn von Holten for good advice.

... everybody at Stabenfeldt who managed to stand periods of e-mail bombing ☺.

... my family – for managing to stand me at all!

A very special thank you to Kit Rasmusen who read the text and answered thousands of questions.

(If I were a horse, I'd like to live in your stable!)

Malin Stehn